TEARS OF THE SON

Tears

of the Son

An Unthinkable Nightmare

R. T. PAGE

First paperback edition 2023

Book design by Publishing Push

978-1-80541-190-1 (paperback)
978-1-80541-191-8 (ebook)

Contents

I couldn't believe what was happening. I was locked up in a dark basement without any water, without any food. Just alone with my thoughts. I felt so vulnerable, so exposed. I didn't think I would make it out alive. Why did she do this to me? Why did she hate me? All I ever did was love her and it was unrequited.

Introduction

Mary Collins is now a grown-up woman in her forties. She is still coming to terms with the traumatic childhood she suffered at the hands of her mother. She grew up in a single-parent household burdened by pedantic rules, oppression and torture. She has always felt alone and misunderstood, wondering how someone could be so evil as to be inimical and menacing towards her and her siblings. Mary has suffered in silence for over 18 years. She lived in a small town in America in the state of Mississippi, also known as Magnolia State, which is bordered to the north by the beautiful Tennessee, to the east by Alabama, to the south by the Gulf of Mexico, to the southwest by Louisiana and to the northwest by Arkansas. Mary grew up in a small town called Raymond which today has just under 2000 residents. There's a lot of history in the town, namely the historic square, the Hinds County Courthouse, several antebellum buildings and Raymond Military Park. It's a quiet little town that boasts a lot of historic architecture and is home to a small close-knit community.

This story is about the pain and anguish Mary has had to endure at her mother's hands, what she went through and how it's shaped her life today. She still has sleepless nights and nightmares when she thinks about her experiences. Her mother's actions were egregious and shocking but Mary still has a positive attitude and is especially protective over her two children, Bobby and Emily, as a result. Today,

Mary is married to her childhood sweetheart, Tony Matthews, who she has been with for over 20 years now. They have moved to Indiana where Mary is now a lawyer and Tony is still a landscaper but occasionally moonlights as a handyman. They live with their two children.

If you looked from the outside in, you wouldn't be able to grasp the pain that she went through but Mary is telling her story so that she can raise awareness and help anyone who has suffered the same fate as she and her siblings did. Every day she lives with it, the shame, even the guilt and it's incessant. She has been suicidal many times but even that wasn't possible such was her mother's cruelty towards her. Mary now runs a small group for women and men who were abused as children and also makes it possible for victims to contact her if they are currently going through the same sort of thing. It's shocking how common this type of thing is. Understandably, a lot of young children who are abused are secluded from the outside world but Mary has a website and even hands out flyers in small communities to reach out to people who are suffering.

Chapter 1

Here I am today, a woman who has been subjected to years and years of abuse. But I haven't let it define me. I've chosen to do something good with it. I want to help others who feel trapped and isolated because it can be a very dark place to be in. So much pain, so much suffering, so much disappointment and betrayal. I still have nightmares sometimes. I have some sleepless nights and I am only now beginning to feel safe, as throughout my childhood I never knew what being safe felt like. Every day, I was vulnerable and in danger, hated and rejected. I didn't know what being loved felt like. The quintessential part of being a child is to know how much your parents love you but I never had that and neither did any of my siblings. I'm still trying to figure out what my identity is today because I never really had one. I was a mistake and I still believe that, but I now use my life as a vehicle to help other people who are going through things that are similar to what I went through. I find it difficult to trust people, particularly women. I don't have any close friends even now after all this time; just acquaintances. I work as a criminal lawyer but also started up a small company that helps to rehabilitate adults who suffered abuse as children. It also offers a helping hand to children who have reported abuse in their homes. I use my experience and knowledge about what it can feel like to be trapped and imprisoned in your own home. I employ many different exercises that can help children and adults cope with their affliction. I'm now happily married to my husband Tony and we have two children, Emily and Bobby. We live in the state of Wisconsin now, north of where I grew up in Mississippi. Tony is very loving and he dotes on me every day. He is truly the reason I can wake up every day, be positive and look forward to the future. As for my kids, well, they give me a reason to live. They are so amazing and I'm so lucky to have them. I give them all the love that my mother failed to give me as a child. I suffer from PTSD. I am on medication and have been for years but I am trying to wean myself off it. Over the years, I did put on some weight; it's what I did to cope and deal with the depression, but, in a way, it also exacerbated my depression. I take each day as it comes and I take nothing for granted. Life is short and I believe if you aren't born to do something, you are born to give something.

It all began a long, long time ago. I must have been about five years old, with frizzy blonde hair and wide eyes, when I first started to notice that something wasn't quite right. I was the eldest of four siblings living in a quiet town where everyone knew everyone. You couldn't sneeze without everyone knowing about it, but my family could. My mother kept to herself. She didn't interact with people in the community. She was blonde, petite, had blue eyes and a beehive sort of hairdo with a fringe plastered to her forehead. In my opinion, she was pretty but she definitely didn't have the personality to match it. It would just be us and her at home all day, every day. We didn't go anywhere or see anyone. We didn't have friends, we didn't go to the parks, we didn't even go to the hospital when we fell ill. For the most part, we were desolate and cut off from society. As I said, I was the eldest of four. The youngest was my little brother Timmy, who was slightly podgy, or should I say stocky – boisterous and very measured, then there was Elizabeth

(Lizzy) who was very small and petite – a bit like my mother, she had brown hair, brown eyes and had a mole on the left side of her cheek. Then there was Sally who was my Irish twin – we were very alike; we both had an aura of mystery around us and were what I would call misfits but we were extremely close; and finally, there was me. From the outside looking in, we would most probably appear to the average person as a normal, functional and happy family but if you believed that, you couldn't be further away from the truth. My family was full of darkness and evil, and it was my mother Susanne who was responsible for that being the case. My dad left us when I was about 5 years old and, just after that, my little brother Timmy was born. My father Barry didn't want anything to do with us but I do talk to him today, on occasion. He is still very estranged and has a second family with whom he lives in Colorado.

I remember that my mom was always very strict. She would often wake us up in the morning at ridiculous hours. She would walk around the house and bang a wooden spoon on a pan or pot to abruptly wake us up. It was relentless. It was what I imagine it's like in the military. What made it worse is that most nights, none of us would even be able to sleep due to the fear of what lay ahead on the next day. I often remember being in bed, tossing and turning and constantly playing with my fingers because of the fear of what would come the next day. I was always restless. I can't remember a time when my mother wasn't cruel towards us, particularly myself and Sally. I don't know why she was the way she was but she definitely had a mean streak in her. I often wondered if it was because she was ill-treated by her own parents whilst growing up but she never alluded to that being the case. As I said, my mom would abruptly wake us up almost every morning, barring the days when she had had too much to drink the night before. It was all I'd ever known so it's only these days that I realise how wrong that sort of behaviour was. She treated us like dirt, her kids; she hated us. I even recall that on some mornings, my mom would wake me and Sally up by pouring water on our faces. This was before Timmy and Elizabeth were born.

I don't have any good memories of my mother. We never celebrated birthdays, we could never discuss mother-daughter things like our first boyfriends, our first crush, periods, etc. Everything was done my mother's way. I was about 5 years old when I remember the first time my mom beat me. My dad had already left us and my mom was a couple of months pregnant with Timmy. I don't have many memories of my father. The times I do remember, my mother and he would be engaged in loud acrimonious arguments that seemed to go on all night. He would then walk out for weeks on end, probably to one of his mistresses' houses, but I don't know. He wasn't a real father and I don't remember him ever hugging me or kissing me and telling me that he loved me. He wasn't evil but he was negligent. Sometimes I used to wish that I hadn't been born. All I and my siblings ever did was suffer. It was like a road to perdition; a life of torment and abuse. My mom beat me so bad the first time. All I had done wrong was come downstairs one night because I couldn't sleep and turn the television on for just a few minutes. She came downstairs and berated me for having done so. She grabbed me by the ear and escorted me back to my room, the room that I shared with Sally, and she literally picked me up by the shoulders and threw me back into bed. I hit my head on the headboard and it bounced off it onto the pillow like a ball. Sally abruptly woke up as she was startled by the loudness of my mom's voice. She clenched her duvet in fear and pleaded with my mom to stop beating me. My mother told her to shut up or she would get it too, so she remained quiet. Sally started crying and lifted the duvet over her head. Her hair was frazzled and most of it covered her little face. My mother told me that I would be punished more the next day – as if I hadn't already been punished enough. I was trembling with fear. She left the room in a huff and I didn't sleep a wink. The next day was foreboding. I didn't know what to expect but I was so afraid. This was the first time my mother had hit me. I always knew she was strict but I never believed she would actually put her hands on me. This was a sign of what was to come.

The next day, we were woken up by loud music that my mother had decided to blare out. I'm sure it wasn't much after 6 in the morning. My mother marched up to our room and shouted at me to get up and follow her so I obliged. She walked me downstairs to the kitchen area which was, of course, right next to the living room and it was open plan. Our home was beautiful but we never really got to appreciate and enjoy it. Rather, certain parts of my home back then remind me of all the pain I had to endure. My mother then instructed me to put my bare hand on the kitchen counter, which was cold to the touch. She said, "Mary, this is what you get for being insolent and breaking the rules." I didn't even understand what the word insolent meant but I knew it was something bad. She told me to stand there and not to move so I did just that. At this point, my face was drenched in tears. I didn't know what to expect but judging by the night before, I knew that whatever it was that she was going to do to me, it would hurt a lot. She was standing behind me rummaging through one of the kitchen cupboards, looking for something. I could just hear the sound of metal and wood clanging as objects crashed into each other. I didn't know what she was looking for. I didn't dare turn my head to see, although it's only natural to want to do so in that situation. I heard her plug something into one of the nearest sockets. It was then I saw it out of the corner of my eye – the iron. It didn't dawn on me that it was meant for me; after all, my skin wasn't creased. I didn't even fathom that it had anything to do with me. A few seconds later, I could hear the sound of the iron heating up and every so often there would be a sort of click to indicate it was reaching its pre-set temperature. I was crying profusely but it was falling on deaf ears. I didn't dare move my right hand off the table. She kept telling me to be quiet and to 'stop crying like a baby'; those were her words exactly. Verbatim. She approached me from the side gently moving the iron along with her as she did. She told me "This is how God punishes us for our sins." She held me with considerable force and she pressed the piping hot iron against the skin of my hand. I let out the biggest scream. It was excruciating and I can still remember the pain. She held it there for a good few seconds until I recoiled and removed my hand from the table, such was the pain I was in. I still have the scar to show for it. I was screaming for minutes after it happened and my mother didn't even afford me the courtesy of putting ice on it. She just let me suffer and wallow in my own self-pity.

Following the incident, she immediately told me to retreat to my room and I gingerly walked up the stairs clutching at my wrist as I did. I was in so much pain. My screams had woken Sally up. Elizabeth (Lizzy) was too young at that point to know what was going on, and luckily, she didn't have to witness that. She was in Mom's room fast asleep when this happened. Sally immediately came to help me; it was instinctive. She held me and tried to console me, and she told me that everything would be okay, but the harder she held onto me, the more pain I felt. She was four and I was five at the time. Little did I know that this was the first of many punishments I was to be subjected to by my mother, the monster. I didn't exactly feel any sort of contrition about my supposed transgressions. All I had done was put the television on for a few minutes. My mom later explained that at those hours, there was a lot of adult content on the television that wasn't suitable for children, but then I thought, "You don't really let us watch tv during the daytime either". I got into my bed and just laid there crying, my face covered in tears; they were dripping all the way down to my top which was getting soaked. My mother didn't even check on me to see if I would be okay; she didn't care. That's what a normal parent would do, or so I thought. I laid my head gently on the soft pillow and somehow, I fell asleep despite the pain I was in. Suddenly, I could hear my mom talking to Lizzy and Sally in the distance, shouting, scolding them as usual. I heard her call my name. "Mary! Mary, get your butt up now!" I just ignored her. I was in too much pain to do anything. I just wanted to stay in bed. I just grabbed my duvet even tighter and tried to disappear. I then heard footsteps quickly approaching as the floorboards on the staircase emphasized them. I could tell by the heavy sound of the footsteps that it was my mother coming to condemn me. Somewhere in the back of my mind, I was hoping, just a little glimmer, that she was coming to check on me and say sorry and that she loved me. Boy, was I wrong. She got to my door and opened it aggressively. It jolted me, feeling like what I know is an electric shock. My hand was starting to blister up and it was stinging. It started to suppurate. The pain was unbearable. My mom did nothing to alleviate it either. She was a mean piece of work. She started yelling at me to come downstairs and sit at the table. I wondered what awaited me downstairs. What she had done to me was such a shock to the system that it had an effect on me – it put a deep feeling of dread in my heart. I remember finally getting up and my mom ordered me to the bath so that she could bathe me. I carefully ambled over to the bathroom which was always clean but had a few mouldy stains gracing the ceiling. She was so insensitive and rough in the way that she bathed me. She made sure to deliberately and abrasively put pressure on my wound as she did. I had to hold back the tears from the pain I was feeling. You need to understand that I was only five years old but I was simulating feelings children in their early teens had. Baptism by fire, I guess.

It was around this age and time that I started to feel angry and did for many, many years. I was always sad but I just felt angry all the time too – angry with the world, with my mom and with my life. Soon after bathing me, my mom dressed me up and told me that I should report to the dining room in two minutes. I just nodded shakily, not taking my eye off her as she said it, so as to not upset her or provoke her even further. I walked downstairs, grabbing hold of the staircase bannister as I did, and headed to the dining room. My whole body was shaking, both from the pain of getting burnt and the fear of my mother. The whole house seemed eerily quiet and it was like I was walking into impending doom. That incident really did something to me mentally; it broke me in a way. After that, I was always petrified of her. I got downstairs and my mom told me to hurry up and sit at the table. Normally, but not gracefully, my mother would give all of us a full plate of food. Before this point, I had never been hungry or gone without a decent meal. It was usually three meals a day. Breakfast usually consisted of pancakes, eggs, cereals and some small bits of fruit. Lunch was usually a sandwich or baguette roll or something like that and dinner was spaghetti and sauce or rice, gravy, vegetables and meat, chops or chicken. Occasionally, we would be given confectionery, but this was only when my mom said so. Sally was sitting there quietly eating her breakfast. You could hear a penny drop. She didn't make a sound as she was still perturbed by the previous night's events. Lizzy was being fed by my mom but it was like she was force-feeding her and getting frustrated that Lizzy was taking too long to swallow. I wanted to say something and protect her but fear seized my courage. My mom got up and went to the kitchen. Little did I know but she was dishing up my food for me. I sat there like a ravenous creature. I remember being so hungry, licking my lips whilst my tummy was doing somersaults and thinking that even though mom was angry with me, she would still feed me as she always had before that point. My mother emerged from the kitchen carrying a plate of food with her. I assumed it was for me. She dropped it in front of me but she dropped it so hard that what was on the plate almost completely fell off. It was half a slice of burnt toast; that was all she had given me. I felt indignant but I didn't dare challenge her. She said in a very stern voice, "You better eat that and don't complain!" I said nothing, so using my left hand, I grabbed the black piece of toast and just nibbled on it. I tried my hardest to not show that I was in pain to avoid upsetting her. It tasted disgusting, and as soon as I was finished eating it, I remember that my stomach was still rumbling. I just assumed that she was still angry with me and it was part of the punishment from the day before. So, I took it without protest. Suddenly, out of nowhere, my mother ordered me to sit in the corner of the kitchen and not to move until she said I was allowed to. I proceeded to the kitchen and didn't say a word. Dressed in my pyjamas, I planted my bottom on the cold, slightly dirty floor and didn't move.

About four hours later, my mom, Sally and Lizzy were all at the dining table again, this time eating lunch. I was ignored and disregarded as if I wasn't there. I could feel Sally's eyes on me but I didn't want to make eye contact with her as I knew she would have felt terrible. They ate and my mom didn't utter a word to me. I just heard her snarling a few times when she walked past me. A few hours passed again and I was still sitting on the kitchen floor, my butt felt numb and sore. My mom was downstairs with my sisters just sitting there doing nothing. I guess like John Lennon said, "Time you enjoy wasting is not wasted time." I was startled because the phone suddenly started ringing. I could feel it vibrating through my body with each ring. My mother got up and scurried over to answer it. She had received a phone call and was on the phone for hours not even heeding my plight. I think she was talking to what I now understand was her 'male' friend.

More time passed; it was getting dark. I was so hungry and destitute. My mom came to the kitchen and started preparing dinner for herself, Sally and Lizzy. She didn't even ask me if I was ok. In fact, since I had started sitting in the corner, I had moved a little bit as my bum became even more sore – so she kicked me so hard and instructed me to get back into the corner and to keep my head down, so I did. I pressed my chin on my chest and I faintly started crying but didn't want to be too loud. I needed an out, a friend, another adult who I could confide in. I didn't have any of that. It was like a dark shadow followed me and my siblings everywhere we went. What made it worse is that she cooked my favourite French fries and burgers. It's like she deliberately did that to rub salt into my wounds and kick me whilst I was down. Pun intended. The smell of the food made me salivate. Whilst they were eating, Sally had accidentally dropped some of her French fries on the floor. My mother instantly exploded into a tirade of insults and verbal abuse toward my little sister but I couldn't do anything to help her; I was frozen. She kept calling her stupid, useless and pathetic. She then proceeded to inflict punishment on Sally. I kept thinking that I was happy Lizzy was very young so that probably spared her from any abuse; well, that was until she got a bit older. She instructed Sally to immediately get in the bath. Sally kept crying, saying, "No, Mummy, please, no!" My mother dragged her by the hair and the right arm up the stairs whilst she left bemused Lizzy downstairs. I wasn't upstairs but I could hear her telling Sally to strip. I was so scared for her. I had no idea what my mom was going to do to her but I could only imagine. From what Sally later told me, my mom forced her to sit in an ice-cold bath for a length of time. I could hear Sally moaning and pleading with my mother to let her out. The screams still give me chills to this day. What made it worse is that there was nothing I felt I could do to help her. After what felt like an eternity, Sally's screams suddenly quietened down and withered away. I didn't know if she was okay or not. I wanted to go upstairs to check on her but I couldn't. The next thing was that I heard some water splashing and then heard my mom insulting her again. I now know she took her out of the bath, picked her up and purposefully threw her on her bed. Then she slammed the door shut and told her she didn't want to see or hear her until the morning. Mom came downstairs to finally relieve me of my punishment. I hadn't eaten, I was cold and I was shaking but she didn't care. She told me to get upstairs and not to talk to Sally or else. Soon after, I heard her putting Lizzy to bed and she went to her room. It was one of the worst days I had ever experienced. My wound looked like it was getting infected. I could see blemishes and abrasions that didn't quite look right. The next day, I told my mother about it and she just told me to shut up and be quiet. I was battered and bruised, but I still kept checking on my sister; it was instinctive. We finally fell asleep and just hoped things would be better the next day. As I said, my mother has always had a temper and was always very strict but she didn't start physically abusing us until I was about five years old. I don't know what changed or what triggered it and I will never know. I doubt it was only because my dad left us.

A few weeks had passed and things were still as awful as ever. We would still get berated and beaten or punished daily. My hand did somehow get better but the scar remains as a reminder. On this particular day, I had some work to do from home. We were home-schooled. In the state we lived in, I now understand that it wasn't illegal. You must understand that my mother was an only child growing up. We didn't have any aunties or uncles, you know, to come to visit us, spoil us and take care of us. It was just my mother; she was the only adult that we had around us to guide us and teach us. My mother's father passed away when I was about 10. We never saw him, nor did we see her mother. I remember her showing no emotions whilst speaking to her mother on the phone when she broke the news of his passing to her, she was as cold as ice. When we were older, she would leave us at home to go out to see her mother but she refused to let her mother see us and have any kind of relationship with us. I would hear her on the phone begging my mother to let her see us but my mother never did. She didn't want to relinquish the control that she had over us, I guess, and for my grandmother to see the physical evidence of the abuse. That's what I assume the reason was. As I say, I was home-schooled and I had some basic maths to do that my mother had put together for me. When I look back now, I wonder what the point of us getting an education was if she kept us cooped up in the house all the time. We couldn't go out there and use the skills we had learned to impact the world, get a job or integrate with society. Despite that, I am happy we did learn something. It kept our minds busy and gave us a break from the torment that we suffered.

I was told to answer some questions that were set by my mother. I was given 20 minutes to complete the exercise. I don't quite remember how many questions she set for me but I would say it was at least 20. She told me that I was only allowed to get three wrong and if I got more than three wrong, she would do something worse to me than burning my hand. I was so scared. My mother was so punctilious. She was very particular, especially when it came to us, and, if we didn't do things exactly as she demanded us to do them, she would punish us. It was tyrannical; she was despotic and oppressive. I couldn't even focus on the questions I had to answer. I was trembling and having a nervous breakdown. My hand was unsteady as I was writing to the point where I wouldn't be able to write the entire number down clearly. It was broken up. I just kept my head down and knew that I had to get it done at all costs. I didn't want to feel my mother's wrath. I knew what she was capable of now and I wanted no part of it. She walked away briefly and left me to answer the questions. Can you believe she set a timer on her wristwatch? I heard it chime and my heart almost stopped because I hadn't quite finished, so, without her looking, I quickly scribbled down a random sequence of numbers to at least show that I had finished. I thought I'd rather show that I did finish within the set time and get stuff wrong than run out of time and not finish at all. Who was I kidding? I was doomed either way! My mom grabbed the paper from under my hands and told me to sit there and not to move as she went to sit on our large sofa in the living room and meticulously check my answers. She made a point of saying each question and answer out loud. "Correct… correct…" So far, I was doing okay. I kept hearing, "That's correct" to which I sighed a deep breath of relief. To be honest, she almost sounded annoyed when I kept getting things right. I got the next question wrong and my mother made a point to chastise me for it. She warned me that I only had two chances left to get questions wrong, I was so afraid.

She then got to question 15. At this point, I had only got one wrong but I had five left to go and I knew that the last three answers were just random. "Wrong" – she had a mirthful smile on her face, almost taunting me as she knew she would have the opportunity to punish me again. Her presence was baleful and noticeable. It was now down to the last three questions. "Question 18," she said and I immediately felt my heart drop to my stomach. I didn't understand what it was back then but today I know it was that familiar feeling of dread that I felt before my mother was about to hurt me. "Wrong. Come here," she said in a stern voice. I got up slowly and walked towards her with my head down. She said, "I'm going to give you three options for punishment and you have to pick one". I began crying, pleading with her to have mercy on me and forgive me. She had a menacing smile on her face; she felt nothing and didn't even flinch. The first option for punishment was to stand barefoot on broken glass for an hour. The second option was to pour boiling water on Sally's leg and the final option was to have her beat me with a belt. I chose the last op-tion; I didn't even hesitate. I already knew that I wouldn't have let her hurt Sally if it had anything to do with me. Standing on broken glass sounded horrific and extremely painful. So, I opted for the option that I kind of believed would be the least painful. But I knew it would hurt, regardless of it being the better option of the three. She told me to wait there as she quickly scurried upstairs, holding her dress as she did. She went to retrieve her belt before quickly returning downstairs. She almost seemed excited at the prospect of beating me, she was so insouciant about it; she didn't feel any guilt whatsoever. Lizzy, who was two at the time, was extremely obstreperous so I worried about how mom would deal with her as she got older. She was sitting next to my mother the entire time this exchange had taken place. Sally was upstairs locked in a closet because she had given Mom some attitude earlier on. If Timmy could have seen the world he was about to come into, he wouldn't have come at all. Poor thing. I remember thinking that all children were treated this way and it was just the way life was. I didn't know any different until a lot later on.

My mother stood over me. I could hear her breath, slow and steady... danger was looming. She instructed me to turn around and put my hands on the wall. The wall was so cold that my little hand felt as if it froze as soon as I touched it. She told me that if I screamed or cried, she would hit me harder and harder. I asked her how many times she would hit me and she said 10 times. She even had the cheek to say I was lucky it wasn't more. I asked her why she hated me so much – she took her eyes off me – her head dropped and she just laughed and told me to shut up. She looked up again and I knew she meant business. She cocked her arm back and arched her back and leaned in with the first hit. It hurt like you couldn't imagine. She would land each blow slowly and purposefully to let the pain fester and just when I could tolerate the pain, she would hit me again just to shock my system. The worst part was that she was hitting me with the buckle bit. It stung so much and the bruises were noticeable. There was a stinging sensation all over my back and it lasted for days. I couldn't even lay on my back without grimacing. It was excruciating. When my mom finished beating me, I just collapsed to the floor and sat there and cried. Things were only going to get worse and I was to be a perpetual victim.

Chapter 2

Some time had passed and it was my birthday. I was turning six years old. Timmy was now born and was a few months old; a midwife had come to the house to deliver him. My mom didn't even hold him when he was first born – as soon as she gave birth, she went back into her angry state. I often wondered in my teen years if anyone even knew that we existed... if we were on the database or anything like that. I don't trust that my mom would have told anyone about us. So far as I knew, only my dad and her mother knew about us. I was expecting to have a nice day, a cake and just a good all-round celebration. But it was anything but that. My mother made me do all the house chores. I had to sweep the floor and clean the bathroom and kitchen. I didn't even get to enjoy my birthday. We never really celebrated birthdays like that. My mother would just tell us what days our birthdays were and that was it – no special treatment at all – no creature comforts, nothing. I went to my mother to ask if I could have a cake for my birthday. She looked at me with complete censure and told me to get out of her face. I was shocked but I wasn't at the same time. She was mean. Why would I expect her to do anything nice for me, ever? But I was defiant; on that day, I was determined to treat myself to something nice. I hatched a plan to raid the cookie jar when mom wasn't looking or was distracted with Timmy or something. A bit later on, she was feeding Timmy in the living room, cradling him but disgusted by him at the same time, so it seemed. She would just yank his head back and forth as she was breastfeeding him so I knew she wouldn't be getting up anytime soon. I got up and stealthily headed to the kitchen. I tiptoed there and, lucky enough, I was tall enough to reach the jar. I stuck my hands in it but I clumsily knocked it over as I was taking the biscuits out of it. The jar made a loud clang and my mom immediately said, "What was that?" I pretended like I couldn't hear her. I stuffed the cookies under my dress and quickly scurried past my mother and my sisters and went straight to my room. "Mary!" she said. "Mary! What are you doing upstairs? Come down here now". By this time, I had already devoured the cookies. I didn't save them or hide them. I got up and briskly walked down the stairs, not realising there were crumbs all over my innocent little mouth. The crumbs were literally falling off my face bit by bit as I descended the staircase. My mother immediately knew what I had done. With her steely eyes, she gave me a death stare; I could feel the heat on my skin as I prepared for my execution. "You took something out of the cookie jar, didn't you? How dare you disobey me; you will be punished". I froze. My mom finished feeding Timmy, got up and aggressively took me by the hand. She pulled on it so hard that my whole hand clicked. She led me downstairs to the cobweb-infested basement and left me there for three days, or at least, that's how long I think it was, Without water and without food. I started crying but this river wouldn't save me. After the first day of perpetual crying and pleading, I just gave up and cowered in the corner and started to imagine living in a much happier and better place. It became my escape in my later years; it honestly helped me to cope sometimes.

I remember a day when my mother had a man visiting her. I'm not sure if it was romantic between them but he seemed very keen on my mother. He would laugh at all of her jokes and break out in a smile anytime she made a witty remark. He seemed into her. I saw a different side of my mother – she was actually being nice to us in the presence of this man. I later found out that his name was Carl. He started to come to the house more often. He had a bedraggled appearance about him, scruffy hair and a thick moustache. He was tall and had dark hair and brown eyes and always wore jeans and a camo jacket that reeked of booze and cigarettes. She had warned us several times to not dare do anything out of turn to him or to say anything that would make him suspicious about the life that we lived. All of us just sat there quietly and Timmy was sleeping of course. We just watched and observed Mom being so loud and so sociable. I had never seen that side of her. It was like she was a completely different person. Maybe this is what she was lacking in her life… a man. Or just someone that she could focus on other than us.

There was one occasion when Carl came by to visit my mother. She let him in and told him to wait in the living room whilst she was upstairs having a shower. I was downstairs with my sisters whilst Timmy was upstairs asleep in my mother's room. We sat there in complete silence whilst Carl tried to engage us in conversation. He tried to ask us what we enjoyed doing, what our favourite toys were, and who our friends were but we didn't respond. I could tell he seemed a bit confused at our lack of social skills. We were just so afraid of saying the wrong thing due to the stark warning my mother had given us prior to his arrival. He said next time he would bring us some gifts and we just smiled and kept our heads down. He must have thought we seemed like zombies. I don't know. But the interactions we had with him were very brief and awkward and he felt it. A few moments later, my mother emerged from upstairs. She seemed agitated but happy to see Carl at the same time. She was so dressed up in a red and white flowery dress drizzled with leaves, a white spaghetti top and perfume on too. She had her hair down and it was flowing and straightened. I noticed that she didn't keep eye contact with him for long periods, maybe because she was shy or nervous. She immediately jumped on him and gave him the biggest hug right in front of us. I wondered why she couldn't afford us the same affection and attention. Carl reciprocated. They embraced and kissed each other. It felt so awkward to witness this. Carl took his hand and seemed to lower it down to my mother's behind. He kind of lifted her up as he did so and drew himself closer to her. I felt so uncomfortable. I didn't know what to do, so I just kept my eyes on the back patio and tried to ignore their courting. I would say Carl was lascivious and aggressive in his manner towards my mother. My mom and Carl soon went upstairs to my mother's room and we would hear sounds of laughter and excitement coming from her room. So, it dawned on me as I got older that she and he were most likely engaging in sexual activity. She would just leave us downstairs unattended. She later emerged from her room, almost skipping as she did, adjusting her dress and hair. She was closely followed by Carl who was walking towards the door. She got to the door, stopped, turned around and almost ran towards Carl, who was lingering behind to give me a big hug. Mom shot Sally and me a cold, evil look as if to say we had done something wrong. He said his goodbyes to us and swiftly left the house. She was waving at him non-stop and almost holding onto the door like she wanted to stand there the whole day watching him. Mom quickly shut the door, smiling ear to ear at him as she did. I had never seen my mother smile so much, except when she was happy about the punishment she was inflicting upon us.

As soon as Carl left, my mother headed back to the living room. She was pointing her index finger at us in an accusatory manner, wagging it left to right as she walked towards us; it was so intimidating. She then immediately confronted us. She asked us what we had said to Carl. He must have said something to her that made her believe that we said something that we were not meant to. She kept probing and interrogating us about what we had told him. She said she knew we were lying and could tell by the look on our faces that we were hiding a secret. Our faces must have been bright red. I just kept wondering why she was accusing us when it was her that decided to leave him in our presence. We had done nothing wrong but sit there quietly and not engage with him. We did as we were told. My mother told us to all get up and line up against the wall in the hallway downstairs adjacent to the kitchen and next to the staircase. Happy to angry in a second. We vehemently protested our innocence but my mother wasn't listening. Lizzy, Sally and I all started crying but I tried to be strong for my little sisters. I had to be brave and tell them that everything would be okay. We knew what was about to come. At this point, she had also started abusing Lizzy, my youngest sister. The only one who didn't get it was Timmy because he was still too young, I guess, but so were we – we were just a bunch of innocent little kids. But my mother didn't care; she was the epitome of evil. We all stood there crying our eyes out awaiting our punishment. My mom went to the garage in an almost hurried, incoherent state which only exacerbated our fear. The garage could be accessed from a door next to the kitchen. I could hear some clanging in the distance quickly approaching. She came back with a metal chain. We were lined up in no particular order, but it was me first, then Lizzy and then Sally. My mom started by beating Sally. For a minute, I had some reprieve. I thought at least she wasn't hitting me first and maybe by the time she got to me, she would change her mind about hitting me, but that never happened. She hit Sally so hard that even I could feel her pain. Sally howled in pain as she received her beating. Poor little Lizzy was having a panic attack; she knew what was coming. She finished with Sally and moved on to Lizzy. I pleaded with her to leave my sisters alone. I asked her why she didn't love us and why she always wanted to hurt us. She laughed in a mocking tone and carried on. I think she hit Lizzy a bit softer than Sally but Lizzy still wailed in pain nevertheless. Both she and Sally were on the floor curled up into a ball and crying non-stop. It was my turn now and I knew I would get the worst of the beating, seeing as I was the oldest of the bunch. The first hit felt like something ripping through my skin. My body was already battered and bruised from all the abuse I had suffered. I'm surprised that Carl didn't notice any marks on any of us but that was mainly because my mother deliberately dressed us up in clothing that would cover our skin completely. It was also the cold season too. My mom just kept hitting me and hitting me. I fell to the ground and was clutching at my wounds – that didn't stop her. She instructed me to get up or she would hit Lizzy and Sally again, so I did. When it was finally over, all three of us just hugged each other and cried together. We wouldn't let go of each other until my mother forced us apart. She left us and walked off to smoke a cigarette in the kitchen. I couldn't quite hear what she was saying but she was talking indistinctly to herself. It was like she was possessed or something. We weren't even told by her to go to our rooms. We were forced to stay there on the cold wooden floor all night and we ended up sleeping there without any warmth for solace. This was normal in my home. Every day was the same. It was very rare that my mother would just leave us alone without doing something iniquitous to us.

A few days passed and my mother had gotten us up early as she usually did. She told us that she had to go into town to see a friend and to buy some groceries and other stuff for the house. I was, of course, in charge whenever my mother went out. Imagine that; I, a 6-year-old, was responsible for looking after her three little siblings. I was a child myself; I was in no position to babysit three little children. My mother didn't care. Everything was always her way. She warned me that I'd better make sure to give Timmy the food and milk that she had left on the side in the kitchen. The milk was already warm too. She also told me that if she came back and the house was a mess, I would be sorry. It's just the way she said it that put the fear of God in me. There wasn't really any food in the house and my mother didn't care whether we ate or not that day. One thing I knew was how to make cereal and make a PB & J sandwich. As soon as she closed the door behind her, I could feel myself lighten up. My lips got looser and my frown was turned upside down and I stopped shaking. I felt a feeling I rarely felt – I had a small moment of happiness, if there was ever such a thing. I made sure that Timmy and my sisters were downstairs all close by and that I could watch them like a hawk. I also made sure to lock the doors as my mother had instructed me to. My mom had a car that she took – I think it was a station wagon. It was red, beaten up and had several dents on it. I made sure to explore all the different areas of the house that I usually wouldn't frequent. I went to the garage, to my mother's room, on the balcony upstairs and I even went outside and sat on the front porch and just looked at the garden. You have to understand that because of the way things were, I was forced to grow up very fast. I did things that I know today most 6-year-olds wouldn't do. It felt so peaceful and placid without her being there and I just imagined how it would be to be without her forever. So, I began to think.

I came back inside and hesitated to turn on the television as my mother didn't permit us to watch it. But I knew I was going to rebel and take the risk. Playing with fire? Maybe – I would turn it off as soon as I heard the keys in the door. When I came to sit next to my sisters and Timmy, they were so meek and timid. I couldn't even get a smile out of any of them. I put on the television and turned to the kid's channel that we loved to watch whenever we did get a chance to see it, which was very rare. I was watching tv, but I was also thinking that maybe I could use this as an opportunity to escape with my siblings. I didn't quite know how I would do it. I wouldn't be able to carry Timmy, but I guessed I could push him in the buggy my mother had. But where would I go? Next door? To another town? I didn't know where anything was as we never left our home. Would I just flag down any random person I saw and ask them to give us refuge? Could I trust another adult as all we knew was my mother and the occasional man that would fugaciously be in her life? I wasn't sure what to do. But I really felt like I had to do something to protect my siblings. I didn't want Timmy to grow up and also have to suffer like the rest of us did. This had to stop. But I want you to just imagine me, a 6-year-old, having the pressure of such a hard decision on my little shoulders. To run away from the person I was born to trust the most, who would love me and care for me... I imagine about an hour and a bit had passed and I could sense that my mother would be home soon. It was then or never. I came to the decision that I was too afraid to even try and escape. Life at home was terrible but what guarantees were there that life outside my home would be any better? Besides, people would probably just think we were lost and homeless and return us to our home anyway, to the nightmare we call life. I was too afraid of it all going wrong and my mother finding out and knowing what she would do to us if she did. I was seized by fear and the unknown so I just stayed and accepted my fate. I quickly walked around the house to check that everything was copacetic and as it was before my mother left the house. Everything seemed okay so I just came back downstairs to sit next to my siblings. I warned them that I would have to turn the television off before my mother came back home. I turned it off and we just sat there all in our own little worlds and not interacting with each other – heads down and all aloof. I just had a bad feeling about what my mother would say when she got back. I thought to myself that if she had a bad experience outside of the house, whatever it may be, she would take it out on us.

I could hear the sound of an old car's engine misfiring as the pistons tried desperately to revolve. I heard the car entering the garage and I knew my mother was back. I felt a sense of angst. Although we hadn't done anything wrong, I knew my mother would find a reason to beat us. She walked through the kitchen door carrying three or four large bags full of food and other stuff. She saw us all sitting there, quiet, and she squinted her eyes as if to say she knew things weren't quite as they seemed. She called my name and said, "Mary, I hope you weren't watching tv." I took a deep breath and swallowed a big gunk of saliva. I was like a little wet kitten. I was scared and nervous. Then I thought, 'What if she turns the tv on and sees the last channel that was being viewed?' I almost wanted to cry; I had messed up. I had gotten everyone into trouble. It took my mother a few minutes to unpack all of the shopping bags and put everything away where it belonged. She spent some more time in the kitchen pacing, talking to herself as she did. I started biting my nails so hard that some of my fingers almost started to bleed. We were anxiously awaiting her return to the living room. I was so nervous and I knew we would get found out. My mother came into the living room and having grabbed the tv remote, planted herself in her favourite single-seater recliner. I had carefully and meticulously placed the remote back on the living room centre table where my mom had left it before. I braced myself. She turned on the tv and it was still on the kids' channel that we had been watching. My mother immediately turned to look at me. She didn't utter a word, but I know something was about to happen. She just stared deep into my soul and it almost felt like I could see her smouldering, hatred filling her mind and I know she was about to rain down on me in a way you can't imagine. But nothing; no words, no insults, no shouting. She got up and took Timmy and went upstairs. I was terrified. I knew she wouldn't just let me off, as she never had before. She spent a good while upstairs, most probably feeding my brother and putting him to bed. I couldn't sit still. I was just trying to imagine what her next move was going to be. I started picking at my skin, in fear of what my mother was going to do to me, to us. Sally looked at me and her face spoke a thousand words. You could see in her eyes that she was scared. Her pupils were dilated and her face was bright red; I felt like I was looking in a mirror. It made me feel a lot worse than I did before. We all knew what my mother was capable of and she would stop at nothing to make sure we were adequately punished according to her. She would sometimes tell us that this was God's punishment for what we did wrong. Almost to justify her heinous acts, I guess. To me, she was just a bully. We didn't grow up in a strict Christian family per se, but my mom would occasionally give us bible studies and then put her own spin on its interpretation, I now realise.

My mother came back downstairs and the room was eerily silent. I was very careful not to say anything to upset her or to worsen the already tense situation. It was like a big storm was about to erupt and wash us away. There was definitely an elephant in the room and her silence was making me uncomfortable. That's one thing about silence – in a sense, it forces you to speak. I blurted out that I was sorry. I kept repeating myself and kept pleading with her not to hurt us. She didn't say a word. It's like it was mental torture. She put us in a place where we were expectant of some form of discipline when we did something wrong. When she came into the room, we were tripping over ourselves to not manifest that exact thing. I think somehow, she was enjoying the mental torture as if the physical abuse wasn't enough. She still didn't say a thing. For the rest of the day, she didn't utter a word to us except to tell us that the food was ready. We sat at the table and just ate in silence watching my mother's every move, anxiously awaiting her outburst, but it never came. I was in shock. She was so calm that it unsettled me. I kept thinking that maybe she was saving our punishment for another day. This fear stayed with me until a few days had passed without any abuse. It was strange; I wasn't used to that being the case. Maybe things were getting better, I thought. But again, I was wrong.

On this particular day, my mother had a different man come to visit her. She seemed to make a lot of effort in terms of what she wore and how she smelled, etc., a lot more effort than when Carl came to visit her. She wore a bright yellow dress with thin straps and brown boots, her hair was down and she wore a fringe. She wore bright red lipstick and mascara too; she made a lot of effort that day. The man, who was a bit on the short side, wore a cowboy hat, glasses, cowboy boots, some faded jeans and a red plaid shirt. My mother didn't even want any of us to be around when he was there so she sent us all to our rooms. We all ended up just sitting in mine and Sally's room, even Timmy. A few minutes passed and my mother seemed awfully quiet, unlike her usual self. All I could hear was this man's sonorous voice bouncing off the walls and hitting my ears. He seemed very loud from what I could glean. I got up, crept to the door and opened it slightly so I could hear what they were saying. I didn't hear much talking, just strange noises coming from downstairs. I was too young to understand what they were doing but I just assumed it was normal for adults to engage in such activity. The man got up soon after and headed to the bathroom. My mother directed him upstairs and as soon as I could hear his heavy footsteps climbing up the stairs, I quickly shut the door but I think he noticed me. I wasn't quick enough. I didn't dare open the door again because I knew what it could mean in terms of my mother's reaction to it. Sally and Lizzy were just sitting down quietly. Sally was colouring in an old, slightly dusty cartoon book and Lizzy was playing with some old wooden blocks that we had in our room. It seemed like she was imagining building something. Sometimes, keeping busy was the only way to cope in our lives. I heard the man's steps receding as he walked back downstairs. It felt like he was there for an age. We were getting hungry but followed our mother's strict instructions about not being seen. It's like we were an inconvenience to her most of the time. Then why did she have us? I never understood that.

The man soon left. I know because I heard the front door open and my mum shouted 'bye' to him as he left. She came upstairs and immediately came to our room. "I THOUGHT I TOLD YOU TO STAY IN YOUR ROOM!" "I….., we did, Mom," I replied nervously. "Get your butts downstairs now!" she said. She gently picked up Timmy who was crying at the time and led us all downstairs. She asked us why we had disregarded her specific instructions to stay out of sight. I thought we had done something wrong and ruined whatever she had with that man. I knew what was about to come. I could see the rage in her eyes. Her face was bright red and she was spitting as she was talking; she even started to foam at the mouth with every word she spoke. I wondered what her punishment would be on this occasion. Something worse than the last time. She made sure to tell us clearly what our punishment was going to be so we didn't get confused about what was to come. She told us that she wanted us to stand outside in the back garden beside each other. She told us that she was going to hurl stones at us for being disobedient. She said it so casually as if it was normal. As usual, we started crying and just prepared for what was to come. She walked around the garden and picked up some stones that were laying around and almost in one swooping motion, she started pelting stones at us. We were facing her and we did everything we could to dodge them. I got hit in the forehead and the eye, Sally got hit in the nose and lip and poor little Lizzy got hit in the chest and legs. I felt so guilty as it was my actions that had caused this to happen. I'm not sure what that man said to my mom but he must have suggested that someone was upstairs which he wasn't meant to have been aware of. But I thought, what if Timmy had started crying as he typically did? Wouldn't that give our cover away? Anyway, this was our fate.

It was sealed. She enjoyed abusing us and just needed an excuse to do so. Once she had finished hitting us with the stones, she marched all three of us back into the house. We were just holding onto each other and pleading our innocence, almost like innocent civilians in a war-stricken country. Battered and bruised, we walked back inside. She then added that we wouldn't be fed for the rest of the day as part of our punishment. It was a horrible day.

Some time passed; things weren't getting any better. At this point, I had come to accept that this was the life I had been destined to live. Lizzy was seemingly very ill. She had a fever and her temperature was sky-high. She hadn't been able to get out of bed for the past two days. I asked my mother if she was going to be okay. She responded with anger and frustration. I knew not to ask again. I kept checking on Lizzy to make sure that she was okay. I was only a child and didn't know what I could do to make her feel better. All I knew was that she required some medical attention. I knew what doctors and nurses were and I knew they were there to help make people better when they felt unwell. I didn't want to suggest it to Mother though. Strangely enough, my mother allowed Lizzy to stay in bed. But it wasn't because she cared that she was unwell – it was more because she didn't care. She didn't even check on her once throughout the two days. That was a job I as-signed to myself. It was incumbent upon me to look after her but I did it secretly so as to not undermine my mother. I kept sneaking upstairs into Lizzy's room to check that she was okay. I didn't know what signs to look for; all I knew was to console her and tell her that she would be okay. Every time I hugged her, I would squeeze her tight, not caring whether I got sick too or not. I would pretend that I needed to use the loo frequently so that I could go upstairs to sneak into her room and check on her. After two days, she did seem to be getting better. My mom did take food up to her with hot water lemon and honey during the two or three days she was sick in her bed. What stuck with me was the way my mother didn't care about us. If we were dying, would she even care? Maybe she wanted all of us dead but then why did she have us? I started to believe that maybe that was the way love was shown. I knew nothing else. Like I say, the real abuse didn't start until I was about five years old and not long after my dad left us. They say hurt people hurt people. Maybe she was bitter about being alone. But she had so many different men coming to the house to see her, so how could that be the case? Maybe she hated Dad and we reminded her of him so she took it out on us or something. I don't know. I was slowly and carefully walking down the stairs after having just checked on Lizzy. As soon as I got to the living room and sat down, the doorbell rang. It was the late eighties, so it was rather uncommon for anyone to just show up unannounced. My mother seemed perturbed by the doorbell as she didn't seem to be expecting anyone. She seemed flustered and unsure of what to do. She just sat there constantly turning her head back and forth to show confusion. She hesitated. She didn't get up to answer the door. Maybe she thought that whoever it was would leave after thinking no one was home. But the doorbell rang incessantly. Soon after the doorbell stopped ringing, there was a loud knock on the door. I heard a man say 'police'. I was always taught by my mother to be scared of the law and the police in particular. She never spoke highly of them but she taught us to fear them. The man repeated himself and it forced my mother to stand up. She adjusted her robe and fixed her hair. She looked in the mirror in the hallway just before she headed to the door. She gathered us together and told us to be quiet and not to say anything if the policeman spoke to us. She opened the door. "Hello, officer, is everything okay?" she said. She was careful not to open the door too wide so the officer could see inside. Standing there, I saw this tall man with a hat on and a police uniform. He looked slightly overweight but very competent at his job. He had a big golden-coloured moustache, wore sunglasses, and I noticed he had a gun holstered on his waist. I immediately felt scared. He peered over her shoulder and I noticed him just as he noticed me. Sally was next to me and Lizzy was upstairs bunged up in her bed. Timmy was asleep in his Moses basket. But the officer could only see me from his viewpoint. My mom noticed him looking at me and deliberately moved her head in the line of his sight so he could only look at her. He suddenly remembered why he was there, cleared his throat and proceeded with his questioning. My mom asked him what the visit was all about. He told her that there was a report of an assault earlier that week. I never knew what the word assault meant until my later years. My mom exclaimed that it was all a misunderstanding. She just said, "She pushed me and I pushed her back. We were also arguing afterwards". The officer, who had an imposing presence, just said okay. He asked her a few more questions about the incident and then left. My mom seemed very nervous as he was there. Her voice was shaky and she couldn't stand still. Even when he left, I remember her breathing a deep sigh of relief. Evil woman! Whilst they were talking, it did cross my mind to run to the door and beg him to take us away and protect us; to tell him about all of the torment we suffered at the hands of my mother. But again, I froze because of fear. To me, it wasn't worth the risk of it not going according to plan. I kept saying to myself that he wouldn't do anything about it, just finding excuses not to act. My mom always put it in our heads that no one could take us away from her and that we would be there for the rest of our lives and we believed her. I was so sad when the officer left. He just left by saying that he was satisfied with my mother's answers and no further action would be taken against her. He even said that she seemed nice and calm and was a good mother based on what he could see. Can you imagine that? It's so easy to misjudge something when looking from the outside in. It was her word against the other woman's, I gathered. Everything just went her way; even this. For someone who caused so much trouble, she never got into trouble herself. That I know of. I heard his patrol car's engine start, then I heard him revving and drive off. My mother eventually closed the door, but for some reason, she stood at the door until she was sure he had left. She glanced at me and gave me a look that said, "Good girl". My opportunity to escape with my siblings was gone again.

Chapter 3

I was now about seven years old. I remember because my birthday had recently passed. Things were bad as usual. My mother would have some days when she would just leave us alone. She still didn't show us any love but she wouldn't necessarily hurt us every day. I remember it was an early evening in winter. I was wise beyond my years and a lot of it had to do with my upbringing. I had to mature faster to deal with my mother. It went without saying. On this particular day, things would change forever. I would almost die. I can't say anyone knows what death feels like but I guess it feels like you may not get to live your life anymore. I woke up feeling very sad; just sad and saturnine in mood. I was tossing and turning in bed, rubbing my eyes as I did so. I don't know why I felt worse that day than I usually did, but maybe I sensed something bad was going to happen to me. As I so often did, I was on eggshells around my mom. I knew the tiniest things could set her off. Sometimes just her bad mood alone would make her do horrible things to us. On this day, she was in the worst mood I think I can ever recall. She woke us up early in the morning. She gave us a mouldy breakfast and that tasted funny. Just the sight of us set her off. Even though we were sitting quietly being imperceptible, she still gave us a hard time, especially me. The day seemed to take forever to pass by. Minute by minute, hour by hour. I remember sitting in the kitchen by myself, not harming anyone, just sitting there. Everyone else was in the living room. My mother was watching her favourite daytime television shows, not even remotely bothered by the fact that she had kids who also wanted to watch kiddy programmes. But it didn't matter to her. She always put herself first. We were just an albatross around her neck. My mother came into the kitchen and she seemed to have a bone to pick with me. She approached me in a slow precise walk, each step she took towards me more menacing than the one before it. She lifted her hand up and just shoved me in the head and my head rocked to the side. She was a bully. She asked me what I was doing in the kitchen and not sitting with them. I just said nothing. I didn't want to say the wrong thing, so, I didn't say anything. She just kicked me so hard in the leg and repeated herself. Then she said, "You think you are too good to sit with the rest of us?" I knew something bad was going to happen. She was in the mood for it. She told me to get up and follow her. So, I obliged. She led me to the basement of the house and I didn't understand why. Yes, she had made me stay there a few times as punishment but I wasn't quite sure of what her intentions were this time. Also, I was surprised that she took me there alone. I was so nervous at this point. Little did I know this was to be the worst day of my life. She shoved me onto the floor and, as I fell, my head hit the dusty floor. She started mocking me by making fun of me and then insulting me. She spat at me and told me she hated me and that I was an abomination. The saliva was dripping down my face as I tried to wipe it away. I didn't know what that word meant but I will never forget her using it that day. It was like I was an animal. She did the worst things to us. She grabbed me by the hair, then she tugged on it almost like she wanted to rip it off my scalp. I was trying my best to protect myself but the more I did, the harder she yanked on my hair and dragged me around the floor. I was screaming and pleading with her to stop but she didn't care, she just carried on. When I looked up at her, she had a look of pure evil in her eyes. It's like she was possessed. It was like her blood was molten lava and it was coursing through her veins. She let go of me and I dropped to the floor. I cowered and was shivering and crying profusely. I couldn't stop crying. I heard Sally open the door to the basement to say, "Stop it!" to my mother but she just told her to "go away!" My mother found an old wooden stick in the basement and continued with her onslaught. With every hit I got, I would howl. She hit me so hard that I started feeling dizzy. She kept at it and it felt like she would never stop beating me. She finally stopped and I believe I must have passed out because of the pain because I woke up down there without my mother being present. I tried to stand up but I couldn't. My body felt weak and sore. I summoned up the strength somehow to pull myself to the staircase and leaned against it. I slumped over and just held onto the bottom step. I was broken; I was defeated. A forlorn figure just there, cold, and covered in wounds. It felt like dying. This had to be worse. I heard footsteps; they sounded like thunder and my mother came back like lightning ready to strike. She was carrying a chain and padlock. There was a sort of pillar in the middle of the basement that she tethered me to. She did it with such satisfaction and she told me that I was to stay there until I had learned my lesson. What lesson I don't know. I couldn't do anything right by her. I was always wrong and thus always damned. She left me there for at least five months. I didn't wash. She occasionally brought me food, usually once a day, but sometimes once every other day. I lost track of time. If I was cold, it didn't matter. I just had to stay there and fall asleep on the 'funky' floor. I remember that on some days, Lizzy and Sally would briefly come to check on me to see if I was okay. At some point, I started to believe that I would never get out of that situation. It was the worst experience ever. Because I hadn't washed. I smelled so bad too. The room was filled with a putrid smell. One day, I just sat there and just cried. Imagine that; me, an innocent 7-year-old being punished for simply being alive. I hadn't done anything wrong. I often wondered if there was a God, the one my mother had always taught us about, and that he must have been evil. Why would he want my mother to do this to us on such a regular basis? It was wrong by all accounts. Being the oldest, I often got blamed for things – I was sort of the scapegoat a lot of the time. One day, my mother came downstairs to the basement. She carefully and meticulously descended the stairs, and the smirk on her face got wider and wider as she did. She told me that I stunk and that I would never come back upstairs. She only came downstairs to bring me some food. I guess she didn't want me to die; she wanted me to suffer. I wondered what was worse. She just dropped the food on the floor – it was some mucky porridge-looking thing that she gave me and she didn't even give me a spoon to eat it with. She made a facetious comment and swirled around and left me. I quickly lifted my head up, scooted over and grabbed the bowl as quickly as I could. I stuffed my face so much so that there were remnants of food dripping down my chin. I was like an animal. In a way, I kind of preferred it too when I think about it. Just to have to see less of her. I did miss my siblings. I couldn't ensure they were safe from down there. I thought about them every day. In fact, for the most part, the thought of them is what got me through.

I'd say about a month in, I started to have a mental breakdown. I would have given anything to have the nightmare within a nightmare end. It didn't. I distinctly remember that I started to feel claustrophobic. It felt like the walls were closing in on me and the room was getting smaller. I just tried to take my mind off of it because it was a very uncomfortable sensation. It was so scary. I remember having several panic attacks; well, I thought that's what they were as I was hyperventilating and felt like I was going to die. It felt like everything was about to come to an end so I can only liken it to death. That happened several times; sometimes daily. I would call out to my mother, apologising each time I did in the hope that she would come and end the torture, but she never did. I was terrified of spiders and one day, this huge spider wanted to play hide and seek with me. I spotted it from a distance – it entered the basement from a small crack in the wall that was facing our back garden. I was petrified. I just kept thinking, what if it saw me as a meal? I had these fantasies of it living down there and growing bigger and bigger the longer I stayed there, to the point where it was even bigger than me. It would overpower me and eat me alive, surely. I just kept crying – I couldn't stop. In this big world, I had no one to protect me. The spider's movement was so scary. It would scurry from one corner to the next, keeping me at a watchful distance, as if it was sizing me up or circling me as if I was its prey. I stood up because I felt it made me look more prodigious and threatening that way. It was a battle for survival in my mind. I was in the jungle and I had to improvise and figure out how to survive. The spider kept getting closer and closer and bigger and bigger as it did. It would disappear and then emerge and then disappear and emerge sporadically. I didn't understand what it was doing. It was very unsettling.

Then it happened. The spider was within about 3 feet's distance of me. It was staring me down, getting ready to go in for the kill. I froze but my mind was still working. It charged toward me and I quickly lifted my foot and squashed it underneath me. I kept stomping on it to make sure that it couldn't move again. It was huge. I was so scared but I mustered up the courage to survive. It was instinct. I kicked the spider away, kicking up some dust as I did and it landed somewhere underneath a wardrobe in the basement. Just like that, the threat was thwarted. I was so hungry, especially after that battle. No, I wasn't going to eat the spider. My mother still did bring me food and water on occasion, or when she felt like it. I looked at my nails and they were filthy and my hair was grubby and dirty. This little incident had kind of distracted me; it gave me something to focus on other than my predicament. So, in a way, it was good. The worst thing was I didn't have any games with me downstairs, or puzzles, or drawing books. Nothing to stimulate my mind. Today, I do meditate but I knew nothing about that at that young age. Why would I? That's when I learnt to visualise and daydream about being somewhere else just to escape the present moment. I would often visualise being somewhere warm and on the beach with turtles and mermaids in the water. I was just a kid, so to me, this was very believable. It really did help me. The mind will protect you as long as you don't get in its way.

One night, I had a terrible nightmare. This was the worst dream I had ever had. It was about my siblings and my mother. We were out at a funfair, just a kiddie's fun world, and we were the perfect happy family. Holding hands and walking in unison together. Timmy was a bit older and so too were my sisters and me. My mother was so happy and sweet. She let us go on all the rides and bought us popcorn and candy floss, and she constantly told us how much she adored and loved us. It was a perfect dream. But then something happened. When we got home from our day out, my mother's mood suddenly changed. She began berating us and saying insulting things to us. She said we were rude and ungrateful and that we had tried to make her look bad when we were at the funfair. We were dumbfounded by her accusations. We didn't know what to say or do. It seemed like the perfect fairy-tale but it was suddenly taken away by the reality of how horrible my mother was. But of course, it was a dream. My mother seemed particularly annoyed with Sally because she wanted to go on a specific ride that none of us wanted to go on. She was begging my mother who refused because she thought it was too dangerous. She made a scene but at the time my mother was equanimous and didn't say anything about it until we got home. Later that day, in the dream, my mother proceeded to punish Sally but made us watch as our own form of torture. It was the most vile thing we had ever seen. My mother started by breaking big glasses over Sally's body, then she angrily picked up her belt, which was laying on the sofa, and beat her with it incessantly. Then she took a broom and shoved it up Sally's private part to the point that she started bleeding. She didn't stop there. After hours of torture, my mother took a knife and started randomly slicing at Sally's skin In any way she felt fit. It was just pure madness and frenzied. We were, of course, pleading with her to stop but she wouldn't listen. It even got to a point where Timmy physically jumped on my mother's back to try and stop her but she just slapped him and pushed him to the side and carried on. We were distraught and in shock. In the dream, it wasn't like my mother to hit us so we were even more taken aback by her actions. She carried on… Eventually, my mom just lost it. She started stabbing Sally indiscriminately. We had to bear witness to this frenzied attack on our sister. I could just see the pain in Sally's pretty little brown eyes. I was so afraid but I was in shock. I couldn't do anything. We were all just crying and pleading with my mother. Sally begged her to stop but very soon her cries were fading away like a distant eastern wind in the desert. We were losing her. My mother finally stopped after stabbing her at least 30 times and Sally's little body suddenly collapsed to the floor. I couldn't hear anything; it was dead silent in the room. I could see movement from everyone but I couldn't hear anything. Lizzy and I walked over to Sally's limp body and tried to wake her up but she wasn't responding. It was like she had just frozen in the position she was slumped over in. Even though I was only young, I knew something was wrong with her. I knew she was dead. I'd never seen her like that before. I'd only seen a dead body on occasion on tv when I walked past and my mother was watching one of her programmes. That's how I learned what death was. My mother was pacing up and down talking incoherently to herself. It was like she was a demon. She was a blight. There was blood everywhere. After we gathered around Sally and were comforting her and crying, that's when I woke up... to my own plight. My stomach was turning and then I immediately felt sick and threw up. It was disgusting, and during all the time that I was down there, it was never cleaned up. Well, the only time it was sort of cleaned up was a few days later when my mother decided to pour freezing cold water over me. I guess that was her idea of a quick bath. She just came down one day and saw the sick on the floor. She told me that I stunk like a dog, so she went back upstairs, came back down with a bucket of water and poured it over me. You wouldn't even treat your worst enemy this way so I never understood why my mother treated us so badly.

I wanted to take my own life. I didn't even know how to. All I knew was that I had had enough. I'd had enough of the pain and suffering. I was just tired of it all. Whilst I was down there, I hatched a plan. I was going to kill my mother. I didn't know how I was going to do it or when I was going to do it but I just knew that I had to do it to get away from her and to save my siblings. The problem is I couldn't do it alone. I would need Sally's help as she was the second oldest. I pondered for days on how I was going to do it. Each plan was more difficult to execute than the one before. I didn't have a propensity for violence. I had only occasionally seen things on tv by accident when my mother was watching it. I obviously couldn't use a gun. I was afraid of them and didn't know how to get hold of one. I couldn't exactly push my mother off a cliff as we didn't live in the hills. So, the plan I finally came up with involved burning her alive. It meant less hassle in terms of being hands-on. I couldn't stab her or anything like that; I just couldn't. I kept fantasizing about it over the next few weeks whilst I was in the basement. It would be warranted considering what she had done to us over the years. I was doing this to protect my little siblings. There was no other way. Running away from home wasn't an option in my mind because I believed my mother would somehow manage to get us back and then unleash her wrath on us for putting her through that. It gave me some sort of satisfaction, almost like something to look forward to. It gave me hope that this would finally end. When I look back now, the one thing that I didn't factor in was if I would have the ability to see my mom burning alive. I decided that I couldn't and that I would simply close the door behind me. The plan was that one day, when my mum wasn't suspecting it, Sally and I would find some gasoline in the house. I know my mother kept some in the garage. We would wait until late at night whilst she was asleep and pour it quietly over the bedsheets. We would then use one of the lighters that she leaves around the house to ignite the flame. We would quickly run to the door and shut it and let her burn. I was 7 years old planning my own mother's murder. Can you imagine that? Put yourself in my shoes; feel my pain. I had no choice. It felt like it was the only way to get out of it. First, I needed to get out of the basement. Over the months that I stayed there, I tried everything to escape, to free myself from being bound. Nothing worked. I was chained up like a feral animal. It was my mom who needed to be chained up, not me. She was the one who was a threat to humanity. I would also scream and plead with her to let me out but I think the basement was somehow sound proof, at least to some extent. That's what I believe anyway.

I had no idea of what time it was. Everything just became a blur. I couldn't believe that I had lasted in the basement for that long. I was beginning to lose a lot of weight. My stomach was rumbling more than ever. All I could think about was food and just remembered all the meals that I had had whilst I was upstairs. Being an adult now, I appreciate certain things that I took for granted when I was young. Things like having a bed to sleep on, and a hot meal. If I learned anything from what I was subjected to in the basement, it was that. I heard the door creak open; Sally and Lizzy appeared in the doorway. They timorously walked down the stairs bearing food in their hands. They brought me some bread and milk. I was immediately perturbed; I was worried my mother would catch them. I asked them what time it was and Sally told me it was 1 o'clock. I asked where Mom was and she told me that she had gone out quickly and left Sally in charge of looking after everyone. This time, she had taken Timmy with her though, which she rarely did. How could she leave her small children at home alone? She just didn't want us to integrate into society. How could she go outside and face people and act normal knowing she had one of her daughters chained up in her basement to starve? I couldn't believe it. You have to be a certain kind of person to do that... just callous and cold.

I grabbed the bread aggressively and just stuffed my mouth. I think half of it ended up on the floor such was the intensity I ate it with but I didn't care. I picked it up and ate that too. I was so hungry. I asked Sally if she could get some more food for me so she hurried back upstairs and almost tripped on the stairs as she did – she got me another two slices of bread and returned with it. Lizzy stayed with me whilst she did and was just stroking my hair and comforting me. I knew I smelled bad but my sisters had so much love for me that they ignored it and just stayed by my side. I grabbed the bread out of Sally's hand so quickly – I was shaking and with each bite I took, I felt better and stronger. As soon as I finished the bread and milk, I was urging them to go back upstairs to avoid being caught by my mother because I knew if she caught them downstairs with me, she would gladly punish them as well. The way I saw it was that I would take on any punishment for my sisters to avoid them having to suffer as well. It was just instinct. My mother didn't have a scintilla of compassion for us. I can't remember once when she felt bad for us or forgave us for being children. She was always on our case from the crack of dawn to the end of the day. Every day. I hugged my sisters at the same time. I didn't want to let go. They were so warm and they smelled so clean. I squeezed them both so tight that I could feel the love and support they had for me. That's when I knew I had to survive for them. We would somehow overcome this nightmare. The truth is, everything that has a beginning has an end. Nothing lasts forever. But when you are in a bad situation, sometimes you can't see the end. That's what the scary part is. But our minds are more powerful than any situation we are in. The will to survive reigns supreme. I didn't want to let go of them but I knew I had to before the evil witch got back home. I just held onto them and held onto them. I could feel every emotion passing through my body. I was happy to see them and know that they were okay. I was sad that I couldn't spend more time with them. I was angry that I was chained to this pillar in our basement. After everything we had been through, I still didn't even hate my mother. You would think I would have but I didn't. I didn't have hatred in me. I was just an innocent little child. It felt like my sisters had been down there with me for too long. I knew I had to let go of them. I rested my head on Sally's shoulder and told her that it would be okay, I then stroked her back and just gave her the biggest hug. Moments later, both she and Lizzy got up and started walking up the stairs. I was just worried that my mother would come home during this interaction I had with them.

Just like that, they were gone. It felt like we weren't in the same house. But it did make me appreciate them a lot more. They gave me strength and encouragement just by their presence alone. I hoped they would be okay and my mother hadn't come home yet, but I would have known because she would have been screaming the house down, and even though I was in the basement, I would have heard her. Her voice is loud. This is around the time that I started to form a relationship with God. The God that my mom taught us about was strict and was an enforcer, but I chose to look at it differently. I believed there was good in the world. I would pray every day when I woke up and before sleeping. I would ask God to protect my sisters and to help me get through it. I would also ask God to make my mother change and ask him to make her start loving us and treating us well. Even though I was still down there, I didn't lose faith. I would pray and pray and pray.

One day, I heard the door open and I could tell it was my mother coming down the stairs. I felt a gush of wind hit me in the face as I prepared to be berated again. I was expecting her to say something to me but she completely ignored me. She just came down to sift through some things in the basement. I heard her snarl at me, "Disgusting". I wasn't sure what she was looking for but I didn't care to ask. I just kept hoping that she would unlock the chains and set me free. I closed my eyes and just prayed at that moment. I prayed that she would release me and that I would be free. It was like she was deliberately taking her time. Maybe she was looking for something, maybe she wasn't, but it felt like she was taking an age. I expected her to at least say something contumelious to me but she didn't. She would just occasionally snarl or make sounds out of frustration. I couldn't work out if it was because she was frustrated that she couldn't find what she was looking for or that she could hear me and smell me. I just didn't want it to be any worse so I didn't say anything to her. I was even trying to control the way I was breathing. I would breathe in deeply and exhale quietly, slowly, and purposefully. I wanted to be imperceptible and innocuous. With every breath I took, I grew more and more anxious. I felt like I was struggling to breathe. I started to hyperventilate but I had to steady my thoughts and stay calm. I just didn't want to antagonise her. A few minutes passed and she was still there. She had moved to another section of the basement. It was funny because I wanted her to free me but I also just wanted her to leave because she was making me feel uncomfortable. I kept thinking, 'Just leave'. Suddenly, it dawned on me that she was cooking dinner upstairs. I could smell it and it smelled delicious. It smelled like roast potatoes and chicken. It made my mouth water. I was like a ravenous creature and would have given anything to eat that food. I could feel my mouth salivating. I was just hunched over, curled up into a little ball and my head was between my little legs. By this point, my blonde hair was more like dirty brown because of all the dust it was accumulating. I just sat still but my little mind was in overdrive. I started thinking about how I could get rid of my mother once and for all. But that thought didn't last very long. I had to focus on the here and now. My mother had finally finished doing what she was doing and she started heading towards the staircase empty-handed. 'What was all that about?' I thought to myself. It wasn't something she had ever done before. So, I found it peculiar. I could hear her footsteps fading away as she climbed the stairs. That sound was like a stone in my heart. When she got to the top, she turned the lights off. I was alone again sitting in the dark and with no one to talk to. My mood was lugubrious and I felt so alone. I had figured out a way that I could sleep a bit more comfortably on the hard floor. I found an old sort of duvet that even a homeless person probably wouldn't sleep on but I didn't care – it was much better than sleeping on the floor just like that. There wasn't much give in the chain I was attached to but just enough for me to move around a little bit and because of that, I was able to retrieve this duvet. I folded it into two and would sleep on it. Of course, I didn't know what time it was but I just felt an overwhelming weariness so I decided that I was going to sleep. I have to tell you, sleep was also my escape; at least that way I could dream and be in another place.

I noticed a bruise on my leg which was really starting to hurt me; it felt like it was getting worse by the day. I just ignored it, what else could I do? I wasn't a medic or trained in first aid and there was no point in telling my mother as she wouldn't empathise with me. I lay down and was staring at the ceiling. I noticed the cracks and the patterns in it. It was a distraction for me. I began thinking about what I'd love to do when I was free from my mother's grip. I daydreamed about being in paradise, a happy place where kids are all welcome and are doted on. A place where there are endless games, cartoons to watch, candy and rides to go on. A place where everyone is happy and where time doesn't exist. A place that has many beautiful bright colours and where the sun shines throughout the day. A place where you can be whatever you want to be. I would often daydream about being in this magical place. I promised myself that for the rest of the time I was living with her, I would never do anything wrong again. I always thought to myself that this couldn't last forever because my mother was an adult and she didn't live with her mother anymore, so I knew one day, I would do the same and wouldn't be trapped anymore. How could my mother just walk by me knowing I was suffering and not even say a word to me? It was like I didn't exist. In a way, I wished at that moment that I didn't exist. That way, she would leave me alone and stop punishing me all the time. I fell asleep. I remember I slept for ages. I just needed to be in another place, another dimension. As I said, this carried on for months and months. The only surprise was that she didn't keep me there for even longer. It was so bad that at times

I would even hallucinate. Once, I thought I could hear my dad's voice calling me. It was unsettling.

One day, my mother came down and brought some food with her. She just dropped it in front of me as she usually did and then she spoke the words I've never been so happy to hear before. She said, "Mary, when you finish your food, I will come back down here and remove the lock on the chain and then you can come back upstairs. You better go straight into the bath!" She said it so casually as if it was just another day and nothing had happened for the past months. Her tone was so dismissive and insensitive – but I was so relieved. I picked up my food just as my mother turned to walk away. I dropped it because I was overcome with emotion. My hands were shaking as I picked up the sandwich my mom had made for me with hate. I almost couldn't swallow my food such was my excitement. By this point, I was emaciated; I was a shivering mess but I survived. I was so proud of myself. I also missed my siblings and couldn't wait to see them. I'm sure Timmy had even grown a bit since I last saw him. I stuffed my face and finished my food so quickly. I was overwrought at the prospect of going back upstairs. I wondered if my mom had changed towards my siblings. I couldn't speak to them to check on them except for one or two occasions when they snuck downstairs to see me when my mother had gone out. My mother came back downstairs and unlocked the lock on the chain. It was the sound of freedom; well, sort of. She didn't even give me a hand or console me. She just said, "Hurry! Get upstairs before I change my mind". I got the energy from somewhere to basically crawl to the staircase. I climbed the stairs as quickly as I could but I kept stumbling on the steps. I was drained of energy but I knew I had

to get there. I emerged at the top of the stairs and my mother shoved
me into the living room and shut the door to the basement. I was back.

Chapter 4

I was a wreck. I was broken but I had survived. I saw a huge beaming smile on Sally and Lizzy's faces when they saw me and that gave me strength. They just laid their eyes on me and couldn't look away – it warmed me up inside. I had to be strong for them and I was. I got up and immediately felt pain in my legs and abdomen. I then headed up the stairs to get into the bath as my mother had instructed me to. Walking felt difficult. My legs felt like jelly – like they hadn't been used in a long time, which they hadn't. I felt like I was carrying weights around with me. It was also fast approaching my 8th birthday, which was in July, a couple of months away. Such was the length of time I had spent down there. But I knew it would just be like any other day under my mother's thumb. Nothing special or memorable. But just a day closer to finally being old enough to leave that God-forsaken house. I began walking upstairs, taking each step slowly and precisely. When I got about halfway up the staircase, I stopped. I just dropped. I could feel this excruciating pain in my left knee that prohibited me from carrying on. I had to stop and sit down for a few seconds, clutching at my knee and massaging it before I got up and carried on again. The last thing I wanted was for my mother to think I was procrastinating and didn't want to wash because I did; I needed to. I got to the door of the bathroom whilst everyone else was downstairs in the living room. My mother was surprisingly quiet. I didn't hear her shouting; in actual fact, she was talking nicely to my siblings which was rare. I wondered what she was up to and what she had planned because it was out of character for her to be so placid towards any of us. Timmy was now about two and you know what they say about the terrible twos. He was also in the firing line, even at that tender age. I opened the bathroom door and gingerly walked over to the bathtub. I slowly moved my hand towards the taps and turned the taps on. For The first time in a long time, I felt good about myself. These little moments of happiness were everything to me growing up. I didn't get many of them but when I did, I embraced them because I knew they wouldn't last long and it would be a while until the next one. I wanted to burn the clothes I was wearing as I'd been wearing them for months and they had blood, dirty skin, vomit, dust and everything else on them that you can imagine. I stood in front of the mirror and just looked at myself and then I began to cry. I had survived. I couldn't believe it. I thought I was going to die down there or stay there forever. I slowly began taking off my clothes and every few seconds I would pause because I could see contusions all over my body. I had an expression of relief on my face but I also thought how could a person possibly go through such horrific events in their lifetime? There was a bruise on my leg that stood out the most. It was large in area and had a slightly purply colour. I rubbed it gently and tried my best to make it feel better but it didn't work. I was just glad to be out of that 'hole'. That day was the day that I decided things had to be different. I took out the band in my hair and shook it from side to side to get all the dust out of it. The bath was filling up fast and I couldn't wait to get in it but I remember thinking it was going to sting because a lot of my wounds hadn't healed yet. However, I was going to enjoy this moment. I stepped away from the mirror, lifted my left foot and put it in the bath. It felt like heaven and it felt like hell. My foot was burning so badly but I mustered up the courage to put my whole leg in. I got used to the pain. I then stepped in fully with my leg and put all my weight on it before shifting the weight onto my other leg as I stepped in with it. I grimaced as it was very painful but at least I could wash all the germs off me. I had to stand there for a while before finally being brave enough to submerge my whole body underwater. I started crouching down preparing myself for an unbearable pain but it never came. I crouched all the way down, sat down and extended my legs as far as they could go. it was so warm and comforting. I used a bubble bath liquid that belonged to the girls that my mother bought for us. I wouldn't dare use one of her plethora of bubble bath liquids. I didn't want to get into trouble just after getting out of it. I just sat there leaned back and enjoyed the moment. I think I fell asleep because I remember Sally knocking on the door. "Mary, are you okay? I need to use the bathroom," she said, to which I replied, "Yes, I'm fine, I will be out in a few minutes." "Okay." There was no real urgency in her voice so I knew that I could take my time and take my time I did. I scrubbed every inch of my little body making sure to not miss any part of it. I wanted to make sure I was clean. I hadn't been allowed to wash for months and months. I just scrubbed and scrubbed myself using my sponge. I added more hot water as it began to feel a bit cold. I could hear sounds coming from outside the bathroom door. It sounded like my mother was moving about so I knew it was time to wrap up, no pun intended. I stood up and reached for my towel and I ended up slipping and almost falling but I held my balance. I stood firmly on my feet and tried to reach for my towel again. I wiped myself down and I could see remnants of blood on my towel but it wasn't my fault. I got out of the bath and put my dirty clothes in the washing basket. I made sure to clean out the bath thoroughly so as to not upset my mother. Once I was fully dry, I applied cream to my body and used some roll-on. I picked up the towel and wrapped it tightly around my body and headed to the door. I felt fresh and clean. I did a double-take and made sure the bathroom was spic and span. It was clean. I opened the door and headed to my room. I didn't see my mom on the way there so I knew that she couldn't have been angry with me because she would have been on my back as she usually was. Maybe because of what she put me through for the past few months she felt bad and wanted to leave me alone for at least a little while and I was okay with that.

I opened the door to my room and walked to the cupboard to look for something to wear. I found my Mickey Mouse house clothes and put them on. They were nice and warm and it was early in the evening, I believe. When I was down there, time became non-existent, so I was going to have to get used to it all over again. The only good thing about being down there was not constantly having my mother in my ear. I know it's a paradox but I was in prison but free at the same time. I started feeling like I was taking too long to get back downstairs so I tried to hurry up. I saw my favourite doll which I had missed and I grabbed her and took her with me. I ambled towards the staircase grabbing hold of the bannister as I came down the stairs. I didn't know what to expect when I got there. I emerged downstairs and it was awkwardly silent. My mother was surprisingly nice to me. She asked me how I felt. It was the first time that I can honestly remember her asking me how I was. She never said, "Are you okay?" However, she asked me how I felt. Big difference. She told me to sit down and that she was preparing some food for us. 'What's going on?' I thought to myself. 'Who is this woman? She isn't my mother. She can't be. If she is genuinely being nice there must be a reason for it. She doesn't have the propensity to be nice.' I didn't buy it.

My mom served all of us hot plates, then we had burgers and French fries, one of my favourites and it was so yummy. For the first time, we felt like a unit, a family. My mother put on cartoons for us to watch and she even had a smile on her face. We watched back to back episodes of Duck Tales and then Thundercats. It was such a nice feeling to see everyone smiling and together and happy. But it wasn't to last long.

The next day, my mother even took us to the local park for about an hour. It was within walking distance from our house but we had never been there before. She did make sure we stayed away from people, however, but it was the first time that any of us had been anywhere. We had a whale of a time, running around, playing and chasing the birds. We didn't see anyone except an old couple and some local workers but no one recognised my mother.

A few days had passed and my mother was still being nice to us, but I guess I mistook her kindness for weakness. Or I just took her for granted altogether. I felt a bit stuffy inside the house and I wanted to wander outside in the back garden for some fresh air. I had already eaten breakfast and felt energised. We were all sitting on the sofas in the living room and my mother allowed Sally and Lizzy to play a board game together whilst I was just chilling, daydreaming. Timmy was in my mother's arms and she was stroking him like he was a little kitten. Without asking my mother's permission, I got up and walked to the sliding doors, opened them up and walked towards the back porch. My mother didn't say anything to me but I know she was watching me like a hawk. I picked up a few stones and was just throwing them aimlessly into the backyard. It was a nice way to pass time and I was getting some fresh air too. I must have been out there for at least 30 minutes. The thing is, from the back garden, there's one little section where you can see further down the road. My mother always told us not to stand near there so we could not be seen. I just sat there and let the wind hit my face. It was soothing. I could hear the birds singing and I was just enjoying myself. I realised my time was almost up. I knew I should have come back in sooner but I decided not to. I was going to take this as far as I could.

THEN IT HAPPENED! My mother suddenly rushed towards the sliding doors like a raging bull and I could hear her shouting from inside the house – it was like a switch had been flipped. It was like Jekyll and Hyde. She was mean again and livid with me. I turned around and saw her making a beeline towards me. She practically threw Timmy on Sally's lap and charged toward me. She grabbed me by the hair and told me that I had disobeyed her by standing near that area where she had told us not to stand. She grabbed me by the ear and pulled me inside. She immediately took me into the kitchen and told me to stand by the wall. Her back was up. I turned towards my siblings and they had all tensed up in shock; they didn't expect such an outburst. They were looking at each other in complete confusion. I tried to communicate with my eyes. I tried to tell them not to worry and that everything would be okay. My mother was circling around me, spewing epithets at me and threatening me. She called me a little cow and a stupid brat. The thing is I already knew this is who my mother was and I didn't let it disappoint me. I knew it was coming at some point. She couldn't change her ways. She'd had so many chances to prove that. I heard the click of a lighter and I immediately knew she was about to smoke. She inhaled deeply and I could smell the cigarette smoke filling the kitchen. It's like she was thinking about what to do next and how to discipline me. With each puff of the cigarette, she would exhale so angrily and smoke would cloud around her face. I looked away; I didn't want to stare into the devil's eyes. Time stopped and I suddenly felt this really sharp pain on my leg. I turned around and she was burning me with the cigarette. I screamed in agony and she told me to shut the f*** up. My mother may have been mean but she hardly swore, so when she did, I knew I was in for it. She did it again and I just recoiled and started crying. I would flinch every time I heard her walk away and then approach me again. She did this at least 10 times until she was finished. I could hear my siblings conferring with each other, confused and unsure of what to do. They were traumatised and scared at that point. Every time she would put the cigarette butt on me, I would look over to them as if to say, 'Don't worry, I'm okay.' My mother finally had enough and just left me there as I dropped to the floor in pain. She headed straight upstairs and slammed her door behind her.

Later on that day, there was an awkward energy in the house. We were all still in shock about what had transpired earlier. Timmy became restless and was tossing and turning in his seat. My mother had been upstairs for a few hours and she hadn't even bothered to cook us any food. Timmy started screaming and I kept telling him to please be quiet or she would come back downstairs. He ignored me and was screaming at the top of his lungs. Mother opened the door and shouted downstairs, "Shut up!" My heart started beating out of my chest – I got so scared that I used my hand to cover Timmy's mouth but he just defiantly removed it and carried on with his tantrum. I didn't know where this came from but something was obviously wrong. My mother's door opened again and this time I heard footsteps, loud menacing footsteps heading quickly toward us in the living room. Like a ghoul that rushes toward an innocent frightened little child, she emerged and then grabbed Timmy and lifted him up so aggressively. She picked him up by the armpits, almost dropping him as she did. She shook him and then took him to the hallway just in sight of us. She started beating him with her right hand. She wouldn't relent; she beat him so badly that Timmy was screaming in pain. She didn't stop. Somehow, we had reawakened the beast. She was back and back with a vengeance. Timmy was trying his best to get away but every time he did, Mother would pull him back and hit him some more. It just reminded me of when I was younger and how my mother used to abuse us too. But he was only two years old. I never started getting beaten until I was at least five years old so I was shocked that my mother would do that to Timmy. His cries just stopped and he was suddenly limp. He just kneeled with his head down and you could tell he was defeated. I think he was in shock. He kept his head down and didn't look up for a couple of minutes. My mother just scolded him and walk away from him. She walked into the kitchen and reached high above the cupboards for her cigarettes. She picked them up and then put a cigarette in her mouth and lit it. She pressed her head against her right palm as she leaned against the kitchen counter whilst inhaling the cigarette. It was like she was frustrated at what she had had to do to Timmy. Maybe she was regretting her actions. She continued to smoke and it seemed to calm her down some. Smoke filled the kitchen and she didn't care. She just smoked and smoked. Once she had finished smoking, she told me to go and get my schoolbooks and that Sally and I were going to do some schoolwork. I felt a bit better about what had just happened to Timmy because at least that eased the tension somewhat and took her mind off it. She seemed a bit calmer when she said, "Lizzy, you are next. We will do some of your schoolwork after I finish with Sally and Mary." I was always excited when I did schoolwork as it made me feel like a normal kid. I loved learning new things too. I went upstairs and went to my school drawer and retrieved some books, pencils and writing paper. I wasn't sure what subject she wanted to take us through so I just brought everything. It was heavy but I managed to carry it all downstairs with me. I walked slowly, one foot in front of the other, being careful not to drop the books. I got to the staircase and had to be even more careful as I navigated the steps. I felt so nervous because I didn't want to drop anything. I did it okay and came to sit in between Sally and Lizzy. My mother came back from the kitchen puffing her cheeks as she did. She seemed exasperated. She grabbed our science textbook and started flipping through the pages. She told us to pick up our pencils and started reading through the contents of the book. She told us to take notes and so we did. It took about an hour I'd say, but I did enjoy it. At least she had no tests for us that day. She told us to make sure we studied what we had learned because she wasn't going to go through it again and we both just nodded. She then instructed Lizzy to go and collect her storybook, the one about the little caterpillar. Lizzy was so ebullient and jumped up and ran towards the stairs. She headed up the stairs in such a hurry that you would have thought the ice cream truck was outside. She ran to her room and got the book and came back even quicker. She was excited to read and enjoy some children's fantasies. My mother asked Sally and me to move so she could sit on the sofa with Lizzy and read to her. We got up swiftly and went to sit in the kitchen so that she could sit next to Lizzy. They sat down and my mother opened the book and started reading whilst Lizzy listened attentively. Only then did we think of Timmy. He was still sitting in the corner of the hallway, sullen and defeated. He had his head down and was scraping his fingernails on the floor. We didn't dare say anything to him. Mom just ignored him and started her reading lesson with Lizzy. A few minutes into the reading lesson, Mom asked Lizzy to take the book and do some of the reading, so she did. Lizzy was about four years old so she was only beginning to read. She tried her best to pronounce the words. With every sentence she read, my mother's frustration with her seemed to grow. She never scolded Lizzy but knowing my mother, I know she was getting annoyed.

Later on, after we had done our schoolwork, my mother advised us that she would give us a Bible lesson. She was quite religious but I later found out as I got older that she used the Bible scriptures to brainwash us into thinking she was doing God's work when she punished us. Today, I know the Bible teaches us about forgiveness, love and compassion, yet my mother's doctrines were the complete opposite. When we were young, we didn't know any better so we just took everything she said at face value.

A bit of time passed and it was quickly approaching the night. My mother went into the kitchen to prepare some food for us. She started cooking and I was famished. She was making pizzas for us – I could smell it. With every minute that passed, my stomach grew hungrier and hungrier. I couldn't wait to eat dinner. Besides thinking how hungry I was, all I could think of was whether or not Timmy would also be fed. I know my mother was still angry with him but I at least hoped she would feed him something. Dinner was almost ready and I was excited to finally eat. Sally, Lizzy and I were all sitting in the living room whilst the news was on tv. We were all like zombies. None of us was really paying attention to the news until one particular story came up that interested me. It was about the arrest of a mother who had killed her five-year-old daughter. She was in the state of Florida. Apparently, she had stabbed her daughter 40 times which ultimately led to her death. It reminded me so much of what we were going through here in my house. I wondered if one day my mother would kill us. I'm sure the little girl was innocent just like we were. I was pretending not to pay attention to the tv because I didn't want my mother to say something about it. She was so engrossed in making dinner that she wasn't paying attention to what was being shown on the tv. I listened carefully. They showed an image of the little girl. It could have been me. She was blonde, had pretty blue eyes and her hair was shoulder-length. Similar to me. I just stared into her eyes in the image and my heart bled for her. I kept thinking, 'How could her mother be so cruel as to want to kill her? What could she have done so wrong that would have warranted that?' I always thought there had to be good mothers and fathers out there. The world couldn't just be full of wicked people. I mean, I knew that when I grew up and had children, I would treat them like kings and queens. I would give them everything that I never had and give them the best possible life that I could. My mother even told me that one day when I had kids they would grow up to hate me and not respect me. She said it once when she was punishing me for something. Those words stuck with me but I was determined to prove her wrong and I have. Today, I have beautiful kids whom I adore and who love and respect me. I don't need to lead them with a carrot and beat them with a stick. They are good kids and I'm proud to say that I have taught them very well.

I wanted to change the channel but then I also just hoped that by the time food was served, the news would be talking about something else because I knew my mother would have had something to say about what they were saying. They also said that the little girl had been subjected to years of torture and abuse. Her mother would sometimes not even feed her. She would beat her and try and blame it on whichever man she was dating at the time. There were some nuances between her and me. She did go to school and seemed to have a social life but she was so broken that she became a recluse. Her mom killed her and buried her little body in the woods some 300 miles away from where they lived. She just left her there and disposed of her as if she was rubbish. I was shocked. I kept wondering why the little girl wasn't brave enough to try and escape. But then look at me – I was too afraid to do that and maybe she was too. I grabbed hold of one of the cushions and squeezed it tight as I felt so vulnerable. I was feeling all kinds of emotions whilst I was watching the news update. It was like a sign of what was to come, foreboding. Maybe it would have been good for my mother to have watched it too. That way she would have been afraid of getting caught if she did decide that she wanted to kill us. I clung to that thought throughout the rest of the evening.

Dinner was ready and I couldn't wait to get stuck in. They say it's very important to make food with love. Most of the time, our food was made with hate but we still ate it. My mother served us our food at the dining table. She went to pick up Timmy as he was still sitting in the corner of the hallway. He was dead quiet but his stomach was doing all the talking. She fed him some food as she sat beside us at the dinner table. The food was so tasty I remember wanting more as I was still hungry but I wouldn't have asked my mother for more in case it angered her. She probably would have called me ungrateful or greedy just to add to the list of names she had called me over the years. Everyone was quiet just concentrating on the food. We finished eating and my mother seemed okay. She wasn't exactly enjoying our company but she wasn't shouting at us either. It was time for bed. I was tired and looking forward to sleeping. My mother told us to clean up our mess and so we did. She had indulged hedonistically in a glass of red wine. I think it relaxed her because whenever she drank red wine, she was always calmer. We headed upstairs at the same time like a herd of sheep. Sally and I went to our room and Lizzy went to hers. Timmy still slept in my mother's room. I felt bad for him and hoped that he was okay. I think what happened to him scarred him mentally. He was so quiet after it happened. He would be that way for years.

Chapter 5

Some months had passed and things were as bad as ever. According to my mother, we were still four pesky little kids that she couldn't stand. The fact that our mother didn't love us was tacit. She still kept on treating us like garbage... like something disposable. I don't know how we had survived for this long with things the way that they were. I guess it was the sheer will to live and survive this nightmare. Being laid back helped me a lot as I was always cool and collected. I was never a rambunctious child like Lizzy and Timmy sometimes were. I realised a long time ago that that wasn't the best way to be when it came to my mother – that aggravated her a lot. Very often, Timmy would repudiate my mother's rules and instructions and that quite often landed him in trouble with her. I tried to teach him to just obey her and listen to her so she wouldn't get angry. That's how I learned to deal with her, although it didn't always work out well for me.

I had been daydreaming perpetually about running away or killing my mother because I was reaching the end of my tether. I couldn't take it anymore and neither could my little siblings. I had no idea where I was going to run away to or how I would kill her but I just knew I had to do something. Because I couldn't imagine being violent, I decided that I would just run away instead and never return no matter what happened. The plan was simple – I would wait for the next time that she went out and left us behind. I would pack a few bags and I would take all of my siblings with me. I would escape and not leave a trace behind so that she couldn't find us even if she tried to. I was vacillating with the idea of leaving one night when she was fast asleep but the idea of being 8 years old out in the middle of the night with my little siblings terrified me. I felt my legs tremble and my head hurt; I didn't think I could do it. My mother always told us scary stories about the dark and they stuck with me. Besides, we were more likely going to get help from someone during the day than during the night I thought. So the plan was hatched and all we needed to do was execute it. That same day, I confided in Sally about my little master plan. I whispered it to her in our room that morning. At first, she was against it. She responded with clamour and frustration when I told her about it, but I somehow managed to convince her to get on board and so she did. I understand why she was against it initially. My mother is scary – you can only understand this if you grew up with me. She has nice blonde hair and blue eyes but she has a wicked gaze that would make anyone a bit nervous. Trust me. She was also very manipulative when it came to getting what she wanted from people, especially men. So, all we had to do was wait for the day to come when she went out to do whatever she did when she was out. Most likely grocery shopping. Then, we would leave her and never look back. I didn't feel bad about it. I was sure Lizzy and Timmy wouldn't hesitate to come along with me. They trusted me and knew I would always protect them. Throughout the whole day, Sally and I just acted normal, careful to make sure that Mom had no reason to suspect anything. My mother's mood was capricious but no one got punished or beaten which was a relief.

The day finally came. My mom told me to look after my siblings because she was going out for a short while to run some errands. We were sitting in the living room when she said this to us and as soon as she said it, Sally and I gave each other a look, both of our eyes were like bug eyes – we were scared and it was like there was a mist around us. We just gazed at each other long enough to realise that we had almost given ourselves away. Then my mother broke the awkward silence. She noticed the look we gave each other and started to inquire about it. "What are you two up to?" she said. "Nothing, Mother, nothing at all," I replied and that was that. She hastily got up and headed upstairs and was moving around quite a bit. I could hear her footsteps through the ground floor ceiling. Each step made me grow more anxious about our plan. I could feel my heart pounding so fast; definite breaths from the chest. I wondered what she was doing but at the same time, I didn't care. I just wanted her to get out of the house. She spent a good twenty minutes up there constantly moving around, never stopping once. Strange. I finally heard her door close as she headed down the stairs. "You can watch some cartoons today, but make sure Timmy gets his food." "Okay," I replied with my eyebrows raised and my lips locked in a smile. I was so surprised that she was permitting us to watch tv; she hardly ever did. Hmmm, I thought. She walked past us and went into the kitchen; she reached high above the kitchen cupboards and grabbed her cigarette pack. She grabbed her keys and headed towards the garage. My heart was thumping through my chest at this point because I knew we only had one chance to get this right. She put the keys in the door and unlocked it. Everything felt like it was in slow motion. She opened the door and walked inside the garage. I heard the car unlocking and I heard her open the door. Soon after, the car started and the garage doors began to open. She reversed the car and I heard her revving the engine and she just drove off. I jumped up and headed straight upstairs. I grabbed one of my small bags and started throwing anything into it – clothes, books, etc. I realised that I didn't have much time so I had to be very quick. I kept on checking the clock on the wall in the hallway downstairs. Tick, tock… tick, tock… it was like the sound of the clock was suffocating me. Maybe this was going to be harder than I initially anticipated. Sally soon followed and started helping to pack some stuff. We went through all of our cupboards and looked for essentials. I then realised that we should have put things together that we were going to take with us before this rather than just doing it on the day itself. I was young; it was a mistake on my part. At this point, Lizzy and Timmy were engrossed in the cartoons my mum had let us put on. They were glued to the tv and I didn't think anything would have drawn them away from that. That was the hardest part of this whole operation, to get them to come along with Sally and me. I just assumed they would say yes without any disagreement. We had almost finished packing two bags. We quickly went into Lizzy's room to find a few clothes that we could take for her. We grabbed what we could and stuffed it in the bag. We then hurried into the bathroom and picked up a few toiletries, just toothbrushes and a few little soaps that were stored in the cupboards. I couldn't think of what else we needed. I didn't know how we would get food but that's where I had faith that someone would take us in and maybe call the police for them to help us out. I had no idea what I was doing but I was doing it. It was now or never. Sally and I headed downstairs with our two suitcases filled with stuff. We scurried down the stairs almost falling as we did. There was still no sign of my mother at that point so everything was going according to plan. I could feel the adrenaline coursing through my veins. I was so scared but so happy at the same time that we would finally be able to leave this hell hole. We got downstairs and Timmy and Lizzy were still engrossed in their cartoons. "Come on, guys, let's go," I said in a commanding voice. "Where are we going?" Lizzy replied. "We have to leave now. We need to find somewhere safe to stay." "No! I'm not going anywhere," Lizzy said. We argued for a little bit and she wasn't relenting. I grew more frustrated because I knew time was running out. I knew my mother would be back soon – I could feel it. She didn't understand that I was doing this for her. I was trying to save them all. A few minutes passed with me pleading with her and Timmy to come along. Timmy repudiated my request – he just said he wanted to watch the cartoons. He was too young to understand what was going on. I could feel a sense of dread. I knew my time was almost up. I looked at Sally – her face looked droopy, her lips were sort of pursed and she had a glazed look in her eyes. Suddenly, Sally started having second thoughts. I could see her pupils dilating, sweat dripping off of her forehead. She was so neurotic. She was scared of getting caught. "What if this doesn't work?" she said in a nervous tone. "What if we are caught or we end up back here? Mother will kill us." She had a point but I had come too far to turn back now. I grabbed the two suitcases and gave one to Sally. I told her to be brave and to stop being silly. I felt like I was beginning to sound like my own mother. Sally reluctantly held onto the suitcase and was ready to follow my lead. I forcefully grabbed hold of Lizzy's hand and she started kicking and screaming. "No! No!" she said. I just gave up. Timmy was ignoring me. He was so stubborn. I tried my darndest to get them to come with me but no one saw the opportunity the way

I saw it and it's obvious they were also scared of my mother. Sally was now adamant that she didn't want to go. She said, "We can go another time, Mary." I was furious that they couldn't see what I was trying to do. I was alone. I got frustrated. I turned and looked at Sally. I dropped my bag and looking her dead in the eye, I told her that I had to go. I told her that she had to be there for Timmy and Lizzy. I walked towards the front door. Timmy and Lizzy were pleading with me to stay. They begged and begged but I knew I couldn't. I didn't want to leave them but I had to get out. I had made up my mind. My plan was for all of us to go but no one trusted me enough to come with me. I headed to the back door as there was a key inside it and you could access the front from that side. I unlocked the door and took a big sigh. I was being so brave I couldn't believe what I was doing. But I was doing it. Sally grabbed hold of my left hand. She grabbed it so tightly that I turned to look at her and she pleaded with me to stay but I couldn't. I used my right hand to loosen her grip and I grabbed my suitcase. I freed myself and headed off. I assume Sally emptied the one I left. I was walking so briskly but I didn't know which direction I was meant to go. I looked back and saw Sally and my other siblings looking at me. I felt a sense of sadness and disappointment but I knew this was the right thing to do. I entered the forest and was navigating my way through the trees and foliage. It was very uneven and I used all my strength to wheel my suitcase along. There was a little ravine that I had to navigate through as well. My suitcase dropped a few times but I just picked it back up and carried on. I started crying – I was already feeling bad for my siblings. I hated the fact that I had left them alone in that house. I saw some sort of animal in the distance just staring at me looking at me as if it knew my pain. I wasn't scared though. As I got closer to it, I realised it was a racoon. It took me about five minutes to make it to the road. I got to the main road that ran parallel to our house. The plan was to flag down any car that I saw and tell them my story and ask for help. The plan had changed some since I was alone. I was now going to tell whoever stopped to help me that my siblings also needed help and that they should call the police for them. It was very misty; I could barely see far ahead of me – just a few yards. It felt so strange being out in the world. I wasn't used to it at all. Every sound startled me. I saw road signs and trees upon trees everywhere. I looked to my right and there were trees, I looked to my left and there were more trees. It was very ominous. I was walking along and I could suddenly hear a car approaching. I couldn't see where it was coming from but my heart started palpitating. This was my chance. I was going to finally be saved. The car approached me and got closer and closer... it was eventually right behind me and moving at a slow and steady pace. Then it happened!

"Mary!" "Mary!" I heard a very familiar but shaky voice calling my name. It couldn't be! No way! I couldn't be that unlucky, could I? I heard the female voice say my name again. Then I realised it was my mother. She sounded more concerned than angry. She got even closer and pulled the car up and quickly got out. I speeded up my pace as I knew there was no way I was going to get in the car with her to go back home. I broke into a light jog, dragging my suitcase along with me, trying my best to get away from her. She called me again and almost sounded sad. "Mary, please stop. Stop! Where are your brother and sisters?" Then it hit me – the guilt filled my body. I remembered my little siblings, having to leave them with this monster, then I just suddenly stopped dead in my tracks. I could hear my mother scurrying towards me and she finally caught up with me. She grabbed hold of me and asked me where I was going and what I was doing. I just froze. I didn't know what to say to her. I just knew this was the worst thing that could have happened. My plan had failed. God didn't want me to leave. She held me with her hands placed on both sides of my face. They were so cold and wrinkly. She kneeled in front of me, staring me dead in the face and told me to get in the car. She seemed calm but I didn't trust her. It was only because we were outside that she was being nice to me. I looked deep into her eyes and I could see the evil inside of her. I refused to get into the car. Suddenly, out of nowhere, another car was quickly approaching us from the opposite direction. My mother started panicking. "You see what you have caused now." My instinct was to flag down this car and beg them to help me but I didn't dare to do so. Why couldn't this have been the car that I saw first? The car was big and black – it was a pickup truck I think and it didn't even stop. I made eye contact with the driver who seemed curious as to what was going on. It was a man. He had a hat on – I could see smoke billowing from inside the car – he had a curious look on his face. He slowed right down as he was passing us but he didn't stop. I guess he assumed everything was okay because I was with an adult, a woman. Things were far from okay. The car passed us and was disappearing into the distance – quickly getting smaller and smaller just like my hopes – I was alone again. My thoughts became clouded and I knew what was about to happen. My mom would do whatever it took to get me back to the house. I could fight and kick and scream but that would just make it worse. There was no way she was going to let me leave. I was capitulating and although I was out in the open, I could feel the world closing in on me. The weather seemed to change... it got darker and cloudier, and everything started sounding more distant, birds, the wind, the trees – I felt alone again. My mother put her hand out and promised me that she would never hurt me again if I came back with her. I didn't believe her, but at that moment, I lied to myself. I looked at her and then looked at her hand. I was dubious about what she was saying. She asked me again to come with her. I thought about food and shelter and my siblings. I finally took her hand and she led me back to the car. I put my suitcase in the back seat and closed the door behind me. I opened the front door on the passenger side and got in and I was shaking like a leaf. I couldn't stop moving my hands and my neck started to feel tight. I felt a sharp feeling in my stomach. My mother was still calm but I knew something bad would happen when we got back home. The car was still running and she started revving the engine. We slowly took off without further incident and headed back to the house. The ride was short and eerily silent. My mother said nothing to me the whole way. We arrived home and she pulled up into the front driveway. She pressed the button for the garage to open and it did. She patiently waited for the garage doors to open. I looked at her out of the corner of my eye and she looked so calm. I was so nervous and scared. What had I done? I was back to this hell hole. We parked up in the garage and my mother slowly turned the engine off, click, click... As soon as the engine was off, she turned to me, moved her head closer to me and with a menacing glare in her eyes, she slapped me in my face. I looked at her with pleading eyes and she slapped me again. The second time she slapped me my head recoiled and actually slammed into the headrest. I just put my head down. "You promised," I said. She told me to shut up and told me that I had no idea what was waiting for me once we got inside the house. I opened my door, got out and then opened the rear door, grabbed my suitcase and reluctantly walked towards the door that connected the kitchen and the garage. My mother just shoved me out of the way – bashing the grocery bags into my head and I stumbled a bit. She opened the door and then it all began. She started screaming at me, saying I was selfish and irresponsible. She asked me how I could leave my siblings at home alone and carry out such a selfish act. We hadn't even laid eyes on them yet; we were still in the kitchen at this point. She angrily dropped her car keys on the table and the groceries she was carrying. She told me that I had put their lives and my own life in danger (as if she cared). I spotted Lizzy, Timmy and Sally who were all sitting in the living room paying careful attention to the interaction that I was having with my mother. They looked scared as usual. I did feel bad when I saw them – I did abandon them, I thought. I was guilt-tripping myself. My mother grabbed me by the ear and threw me to the floor in the kitchen then she started beating me. She was hitting me with fists, not open-handed. She hit me so hard that it dislodged one of my teeth. The onslaught was relentless and tireless. She wouldn't stop hitting me. I just kept asking her why she didn't love us. She leaned over me, grabbed hold of me and shook me and then slapped me in the face again. I fell to the floor again – helpless. That seemed to make her even angrier. I was crying and this time I knew I had messed up. I shouldn't have left them alone. If I was going to leave, I should have left with them. The beating finally stopped and I just lay on the kitchen floor crying my eyes out, not so much because of the pain but more because my plan had failed. My mother told me to get out of her sight. I somehow got up and walked upstairs to my room. I didn't even look at my siblings as I walked through the living room where they were all congregated. I heard a whimper as I walked past them. When I got to my room, I shut the door and just lay in my bed crying. I spent the rest of the day there. I didn't even have an appetite.

I just remember waking up in the middle of the night. I rolled over to look at Sally, who was fast asleep. I felt so isolated and so alone. I was surprised that my mother's punishment hadn't been more severe than it was. I then started thinking. The only other option I had was to get rid of my mother once and for all; to extricate myself. I meticulously thought through my 'Plan B' which was to kill my mother. I was going to burn her whilst she was asleep. I was going to need Sally's help. I knew I had to get it done as soon as possible. I was running out of time and things were just execrable. I had to act fast. Initially, I kept thinking of how I was going to convince Sally to jump on board with my plan. She didn't want to run away with me so why would she want to kill our mother? She would have probably thought it was risible but I knew I needed someone to help me and my other siblings were too young to help. I just lay there and pondered over the plan. It wasn't going to be easy. I was going to be responsible for someone's death. Imagine me, a little child, with that weight on my shoulders. Something I'd have to live with for the rest of my life. But as they say, it's reasons first, answers second. I was wide awake. I had become so hooked on this plan that I didn't want to sleep. I even felt like waking Sally up to tell her about it but I decided against doing that. I was worried that she wouldn't go along with the plan, or worse, that she would oust me and reveal my plan to my mother – but I had to tell her – I trusted her. I was staring at the ceiling. The moonlight was shining through my window illuminating my bedroom; it was beautiful. I always marvelled at the moon and the stars and just the pulchritude of the universe. It's a beautiful thing. I could hear something coming from outside so I stood up slowly and headed to my bedroom window. I couldn't make out what it was but some sort of creature was in our back garden rummaging through our trash. It kind of scared me because I'd never seen that before. Something attracted it to the bin. Or maybe it was just hungry. I was so thirsty so I got up and tiptoed downstairs to get myself a glass of water. I made sure to use the natural light from the moon to guide my path rather than turn any lights on. I was ultra-quiet; I didn't want to wake my mother up. I got to the kitchen and opened the cupboard and got myself a cup. I turned the tap on and let it run for a few seconds before filling my cup with it. I took a sip of the water and it immediately quenched my thirst. I pulled up a chair and sat down and just kept thinking about my plan. I was rubbing my temple thinking over my plan and then I heard noises coming from upstairs. Someone was awake. I could hear them going to the bathroom but judging by the creak of the door it didn't sound like my door; I think it was Lizzy. I remained still and didn't move. I swallowed a big gulp of saliva and started feeling a bit anxious. Whoever it was left the bathroom and headed back to their room. I waited for a few minutes until it was safe to sneak back upstairs. The stairs were creaking so I took each one slowly and as quietly as possible. I would pause after taking each one. When I got to the landing at the top of the stairs, I made haste and just scuttled quickly to my room and closed the door behind me quietly. I was breathing so heavily and rapidly that anyone who was up would have heard my shallow thumping breaths fill their eardrums. Sally was up. She asked me what I was doing and I told her I had just gone to get some water. I figured it was the perfect time to tell her about my plan. The moment was silent – it was ambushed by the sounds of the strong winds, and you could hear the trees whooshing and blowing from side to side – there was another pause…"We have to kill her… kill Mother." Sally gasped; she seemed shocked. She didn't speak for about 30 seconds. She just stared at me with a blank look on her face. I told her it was the only way and I asked her if she wanted to live this way for the rest of her life under my mother's tyranny. I sat down on her bed at this point. She told me I was crazy but she finally agreed to go along with it. However, she insisted that she wouldn't be the one to ignite the fire. She would just be a lookout, so to speak. We agreed that we would do it in the following two days. We would use the next day to look for the gasoline and make sure we knew where at least one lighter was. We told each other we loved each other and we gave each other a big hug, neither of us wanting to let go. We finally let go of our embrace and I snuck back into my bed. We both lay on our beds as quiet as mice. I knew what she was thinking and she knew what I was thinking. I turned my head towards the wall and I was gone.

The day had come to execute our plan. We acted normal and just behaved as we did every day. The day seemed to pass by quite quickly. Mother made us food for breakfast and lunch. It was fast approaching dinner time and I was growing more nervous because I knew what was coming. My mother hadn't been at her worst that day but it didn't undo all the heinous stuff she had done to us and was going to do to us. She went to the kitchen and started preparing dinner. She even asked me to cut up some vegetables for her to add to her casserole. So, I obliged. Holding the knife in my hand inches away from her felt weird. It made me rather uncomfortable. I felt a sense of guilt. I did love my mother in a way but she didn't love me. She tolerated me; she didn't celebrate me or my siblings. I finished cutting up the vegetables and handed the bowl to my mother. She didn't even thank me, she just told me to go and sit down and so I did. About forty minutes later, dinner was ready. It was like the last supper. We all sat at the dinner table and quietly ate our food. My mother, for some reason, was trying to engage us in balderdash. I wasn't interested but to make sure I didn't give myself away, I chimed into the conversation here and there. She was unusually garrulous that day; who knows why. We finished dinner and wound down in front of the television. My mother just watched her usual programmes whilst we sat there bored and twiddling our thumbs and playing with our hair. Timmy was already asleep but the rest of us were still awake. I didn't feel it was right to tell Lizzy about the plan as she was a bit too young, I felt. I know she would have spoiled it. I was doing this for her, after all, so didn't need her permission. A few hours passed and it was getting late. My mother sent us all to bed and Sally and I went to the bathroom, brushed our teeth and just stared at each other. It was like we were talking to each other without saying any words. It was clear that she was still with the plan. We finished up and nervously put our toothbrushes on the rack and headed to our bedroom. I asked her if she was ready and she nodded timorously. The plan was to go to bed early, turn off the lights and pretend we were asleep. We would wait until late at night as we knew our mother went to bed around 11. I knew this because of all the sleepless nights I'd had when I would be up just when my mother was about to go to bed. We also had a clock on our wall so that helped us out. We would then sneak downstairs into the garage to pick up the gasoline cylinders. Then we would pour it into a bucket. We had loads of them in the bathroom. Then we would sneak into her room and pour it over her sheets while she was asleep. We would also grab a lighter from the kitchen drawer on our way back upstairs. It got to about midnight. I sat up and whispered to Sally to ask if she was up and she replied with a tenuous "yes". I asked her if she was ready and she said she was. I got up and put some shoes on. I snuck into the bathroom and grabbed a medium-sized bucket. I came back out and then together we snuck downstairs, one by one, slowly and stealthily. We headed into the garage through the kitchen and the door squeaked a bit but we continued with our plan. We got in there and unscrewed the lid of the gasoline cylinder and both lifted it up and poured it into the bucket. We filled it about three-quarters full and figured that would be enough. We didn't hear a peep coming from upstairs. Side by side, we carried the bucket and shut the kitchen door behind us. I opened a kitchen drawer and grabbed a yellow click lighter. We headed upstairs as quiet as mice. I told myself we were almost there. When we got to the landing at the top of the stairs, I decided that I would open Mother's door a crack to check if she was asleep. I walked over to her room and put my hand on the door handle, it was cold to the touch. I turned it around, opened it slightly and peeked through. She was fast asleep; she was even snoring. I turned back and with my hand, I instructed Sally to come. She couldn't, the bucket was too heavy for her to carry alone so I left the door ajar and walked over to her to help her. We carried it into the room, then took off our shoes so there would be minimal noise just before we went in. Mother was still snoring loudly. We got to her bed and then lifted the bucket above the bed and started pouring the contents onto the bed very evenly and gently. We covered all parts of it. We had to be fast because it wouldn't be long until my mother would wake up from feeling the wetness against her bare skin. It smelled so bad too... a very strong odour. I gave the bucket to Sally and reached into my pocket for the lighter. I gestured to her to stand back. Once she was at the door, I tried to light the lighter. It just clicked but it wouldn't spark. I tried a second time and my mother suddenly moved. She turned over but just carried on snoring. The lighter wasn't working but it was too late to go downstairs to try and get another one. I tried a third time and this time it sparked. I moved closer to my mother and just stared at her as the flame danced from side to side. I whispered to her, "Why couldn't you just love us? Why?" Just as I was about to put the flame on the bed, she suddenly woke up. She shot up like a spring chicken and immediately yelled at me and asked me what I was doing. She saw the flame but it was blown out by her sudden and quick movement – then it dawned on her that there was gasoline all over her bedsheets. She was furious but also very confused. Sally ran away just as my mother grabbed the lighter out of my hand. She slapped me across the face and said, "You tried to kill me!" I denied it vehemently and she said it again. She left me and ran to the bathroom to wash the gasoline off her body. She must have taken off her clothes and put on her robe and rushed back into her room where I stood because I was frozen. I was stammering; I couldn't get a word out. This was the worst thing I'd ever done and I knew the consequences would be deadly. She had already seen Sally at her door so she called to her too. "Sally, come here!" She turned all the lights on upstairs and was yelling at the top of her voice. She told us both to meet her downstairs. We went downstairs crying as we usually did. I don't think she believed we had the gall to even try such a thing. She followed us down and immediately took us down to the basement. She literally pushed us down the stairs at the same time. I landed and hit my head and Sally hurt her leg. We both grimaced in pain just as my mother slammed the door shut and locked the door.

She shouted through the door that we were to stay there until she let us out. I had been there before but Sally hadn't; she couldn't stop crying. Somehow, I knew this was it and that we would never get out again. There was a lot of movement. I assumed Timmy and Lizzy had been woken up by the noise... then suddenly, it was dead quiet and I dreaded what was to come next.

Chapter 6

To our surprise, the very next morning, we heard the rattle and then heard it unlock. My mother appeared at the top of the stairs, still, with her shoulders dropped and her head down. She was in tears. I think it was very early in the morning as I couldn't hear Timmy or Lizzy moving around upstairs. We just saw our mom. She instructed us to come to the kitchen so we walked up the stairs very nervously and met her there. She slid back and ended up planting her bum on the floor. She had her head in her hands and was weeping. "You guys hate me... you wanted to kill me." I couldn't believe she was acting like she was the victim. She very much deserved it, I thought at that moment. How could she be so disappointed and sad? She carried on crying. I'd never seen my mother cry before, not like that anyway. The tears just ran down her face like water does down a cliff. It was rather shocking to see, to see that she actually had emotions other than just anger and rage. A little part of me wanted to go over to her and console her but the other part of me decided against it. I wouldn't say I was pleased that she was upset but I wasn't sad about it either. She had been horrible to us most of our lives. I could tell that Sally was feeling a sense of guilt. It was written all over her face. She looked over at my mother with sheepish eyes. We just stood there and let her bawl her eyes out. We eventually left my mother sitting on the floor, drenched in her own tears, and we went to our room. We gave each other a look of confidence and knew we had got away with it. The fact that my mother only left us in the basement for one night as punishment was shocking to us both. Ever since then, our punishments were a lot less frequent.

Some years had passed. I was now about 13 years old and Sally was 12, Lizzy was about 10 and Timmy was 8. We all had our own bashful personalities. My mother was still my mother. For about a year, she seemed to calm down quite a lot. I don't know what got into her. She just seemed a lot calmer in general. Maybe she became more lenient because we were getting older, or she was just tired of being so strict. But then suddenly, it all seemed to start again. This time, her anger was aimed at Timmy. He just reminded me of when I was that age and the sort of things my mother would do to me. Timmy had his own personality. To this day, he has never been diagnosed but I felt like he may have been on the autism spectrum. He is very unique. My mother had a difficult time controlling him especially. Timmy was rebellious and more edgy and perilous than the rest of us. He was quite big for an 8-year-old. He had brown eyes and he was quite tall and stocky. Well, he was for his age. My mother was not very tall and by the time Timmy got to 12, he towered over her. I remember one day Timmy had seen an advert on tv advertising the new Game-boy. He was so captivated by the advert, his eyes were glued to the tv. They lit up and he started to adjust his posture on the seat as he sat up and almost stared towards the tv. He was determined to get one and became obsessed with the idea. He begged my mother to get it for him, and of course, she refused. He didn't relent, he kept asking her over and over again to get it for him. I thought to myself why on earth would she do that considering how she treated us? She was still a monster. Her physical abuse became more verbal but she was still very vituperative and bitter towards us. A few days passed and the advert came on tv again. Timmy was his excited self; he jumped up and held onto my mother's arm and tugged on it. "Please, Mommy, please get it for me," he said. She shook her head and just said "NO!" in a stern and serious tone. Timmy was disgruntled and upset. It was visible for everyone to see. He sat back down and just stayed there in complete silence. He didn't utter a word for the next couple of hours. His arms were crossed and his bottom lip had raised over his top lip. Food was ready and Timmy didn't even move. He refused to eat anything; it was like a protest. We all stood up except Timmy and headed over to the dinner table. I was famished; I couldn't wait to eat lunch. My mother said, "Timmy, if you don't get your butt here now, you will regret it." He didn't even react. It was like he was beginning to think because he was the only boy, he was the man of the house and what he said went. He looked up at her with indignant eyes and continued to rebel. She left him alone. We were eating and Timmy's food was getting cold. She asked him again and this time he verbally refused to come and eat. My mother slammed her fork on the table and hurried over to Timmy. She was pointing her left index finger right in his face, scolding him and shouting at him. We looked over to see what was happening. Timmy just ignored her and stared her dead in the eyes. He was determined to get his way. My mother threatened him again. He kept ignoring her. She finally snapped, slapped him so hard across the face and yanked on his arm as if to forcefully drag him to the kitchen. Timmy didn't budge. Instead, he yelled back at her and told her not to touch him again. She recoiled and was almost more enraged at his defiance. She slapped him again and his head rocked to the side. She came back to the kitchen whilst we were still eating and grabbed Timmy's plate. She took it over to him and he was still in the same position. She grabbed a handful of food in her right hand and started trying to force-feed Timmy. He had a mouth full of food but didn't want to swallow it. My mother grabbed his neck in a way to try and get him to swallow but Timmy didn't. He spat the food out and it landed all over the floor. My mother was furious. She grabbed Timmy by the right arm and told him he was going to get what was coming to him. She ushered him into the basement and literally pushed him down the stairs before our very eyes. He fell and we could hear him yell in pain. She locked the door and came back to sit at the table. She put her head in her hands and just looked down at her plate. She then slowly carried on eating. A few minutes later, we had all finished eating. My mother got up first. She grabbed some kitchen towels and cleaned up Timmy's mess in the living room. We could hear him downstairs kicking and screaming. Things were falling over and being kicked around. He was like a raging bull. He seemed to have similar anger problems to my mother. Like mother, like son. I knew what it was like to be down there for a lengthy period, but I worried that he wouldn't cope. He was more needy than we were and more impetuous. My mom warned us that if any of us tried to help him, we would get into deep trouble and that scared us. As uncomfortable as it was, we just ignored Timmy's muffled screams and moved into the living room. My mother opened the door to the basement and shouted at Timmy and told him to shut up or he would stay down there forever. He responded by just yelling obscenities back at her. He was so angry; he had so much rage in him. I sat on the sofa and let it swallow me up as I drifted away. I started thinking about the time that Sally and I tried to burn my mother alive. The thought was perpetual and I started thinking of getting rid of her again. I had to hatch another plan this time because that didn't work the first time we tried. I just sat there and closed my eyes whilst Sally and Lizzy were watching tv with my mom. I was pretending to sleep while in actual fact all I was thinking about was how else I could get rid of her. I finally stumbled on the master plan. I would stab her with one of the large kitchen knives in the kitchen. I had seen it before in movies that my mother put on and it didn't look that hard. I just had to hit some vital organs. I would stab her several times in the back when she didn't expect me to attack. This time, I would do it alone. I wouldn't tell anyone about it. Lizzy was so sweet and innocent. She was the purest thing ever and it killed me to see my mother harm her. I had planned to carry out my plan whilst my mother's back was turned when she was cooking or washing up the dishes. I knew on that day it wasn't my turn to wash up nor was it my sisters' turn and Timmy was downstairs anyway. My mom was strict when we got older. She gave us schedules of whose duties were what on certain days. We did the cleaning, sometimes cooking, laundry and ironing. That day was my mother's turn. But I felt the plan was a bit premature and I wasn't mentally ready yet to do it. I was going to wait for at least a few days before I did anything.

A few days passed and Timmy was still in the basement. She hadn't fed him, apart from once when she just threw an apple, a banana and a bottle of water downstairs to him like he was a dog. He had stopped clamouring and was quiet now. He was too young to remember when I was locked down there for months. I wish there was more I could have done for him. Well, there was – I could stab my mother. On this day, I was in the bathroom cleaning up. I also had dishes duties. But my mother was to do the cooking for all three meals. It killed me to think we were eating three meals and Timmy was barely having one. He was a boy too so I knew even at that young age that he needed more food than the rest of us did. It got to about 2 o'clock that afternoon and my mother was in the kitchen preparing lunch. I was staring at the clock just watching the seconds and minutes go by. She had put on some old classic music and was drinking a glass of wine whilst dancing and cooking. She was merry and in a good mood. I couldn't do anything on that day. It just wouldn't be right, I thought. So I didn't. I slept on it. The next day it was Mom's turn to do the dishes. I thought I'd strike then. I would go to the kitchen and pick up a knife and hide it under my pillow when I got upstairs. At around 11 pm that night, when everyone was in their room, I snuck downstairs to retrieve the biggest knife I could find. It was sturdy and very big. I then remembered Timmy so, whilst I was in the kitchen, I quickly made him a peanut butter sandwich. I opened the door to the basement and took it down to him quickly. He was forlorn and sad. He had tears on his face. I put my finger on his lips to make sure he didn't make any noise. I just nodded and whispered to him that it would be okay and that I loved him. I gave him the food and he just ate it like a ravenous creature. In seconds, he was done. I gave him a big hug and told him I'd come and check on him again soon. I left him and looked back once more whilst I was heading up the stairs. I felt so sorry for him. I wished we could have swapped places. I picked up the knife; we had a plethora of big knives so I knew my mother wouldn't notice anything was missing. I went upstairs very quietly and headed to my room. I put the big knife under my pillow and mentally prepared myself for what I had to do the next day. I now had built up the courage to carry out my plan.

The next day came and I woke up bright and early. I decided that I would make breakfast just to sweeten my mother up a bit. It worked. Everyone came downstairs; I think they were woken up by the nice smell of bacon, eggs and sausages. We had a lovely feast. I even gave some food to Timmy because I was able to go down there quickly whilst cooking before anyone came down. He was so grateful. But his appearance was so bedraggled and he was in bits. His hair looked scruffy and his clothes needed a wash. We all finished eating up and my sisters and I walked into the living room. My mother started up on the dishes and I knew it was my time to strike. I waited until I was sure I could hear the plates clanging and then I got up and quickly and quietly snuck up the stairs. I picked up the knife and concealed it under my robe. I came back down and sat there with it unbeknownst to my sisters. I waited a minute, then stood up and snuck towards the kitchen. My sisters were watching cartoons because they had free reign over the tv. They were engrossed in it and didn't notice what I was doing. I braced myself and summoned the courage to strike. I snuck up behind my mother whilst she was singing to herself. She paused and was looking outside of the window. I stuck the knife in her. I think I stabbed her about five times in the upper back region. I would wail each time I stuck the knife in. I could feel her flesh each time I stuck the knife in. She collapsed to the floor screaming in agony. I immediately threw up. My sisters jumped up and ran to the kitchen to see what was going on. They were asking me what I had done. To their shock, I told them I had stabbed Mom. I clung to the knife and could see the blood dripping off of it. My mother was covered in blood. She was hunched over and I think she was losing consciousness. What had I done? I was a killer. I started feeling bad and I asked her if she was okay. She didn't respond. Her head was limp and flopping from side to side as she lifted her arm up to try and get to her feet, but she couldn't. None of us called the ambulance and she didn't ask for us to either. About twenty minutes passed with us just standing there staring at her and each other. No one knew what to do. My mother opened her eyes and lifted her head up. She spoke softly asking what happened. To this day, I don't know how she did it but she found the strength to lift herself up. She seemed to have recovered and was now walking around holding her back as she did. She knew she needed to get to the hospital so she grabbed the car keys and headed straight to the garage. I asked her where she was going and she just said, "This is your fault. How could you do this to me?" I looked down at the floor in shame and felt very melancholic. The car started and a few seconds later she was gone.

I don't know what happened at the hospital but my mother returned later that evening. I was shocked. Wasn't there a criminal investigation etc? Wouldn't the police get involved? Somehow, I was hoping she would at least tell someone about us and someone would come and take us away, but that never happened. We heard the car pulling into the garage and my heart dropped into my stomach. I didn't know what to expect. I thought she might kill me. The door that linked the kitchen to the garage opened and she emerged. She gave me a death stare. She shot it at me and kept her gaze on me; it was menacing. It made the hairs on my neck stand up. Timmy was still in the basement, but we had all gone to check on him before she got back. She wanted to have a word with me and called me into her bedroom. I was surprised by the calmness in her voice. I followed her up the stairs as my siblings anxiously waited. We got to her room and she directed me to sit down on the chair by her dresser which had an assortment of things heaped on it. She sat down gingerly and asked me why I wanted to kill her. She said I had tried twice now and she was worried that I might try again. I explained to her that I didn't understand why she hated us so much and treated us like trash. She of course denied it vehemently and explained that it was just to discipline us because the world is cruel and she was trying to prepare us for life, as she put it. We spoke for quite some time and we were going around in circles. She told me that she didn't have the strength to cook and that I should make fries and burgers for dinner. It was late but none of us had eaten. Because we were talking cordially, I was tempted to ask what she planned for Timmy. I just said it: "When will Timmy be allowed back upstairs? You can't leave him down there for as long as you left me there." She just said, "He needs to learn to obey me and not to throw a tantrum every time he doesn't get what he wants," she said as she clung to her back. It was clear she was in a lot of pain. I just kept quiet. We both sat there in silence for a moment. I felt bad for her somehow. I just wished at that moment we could bury the hatchet and start over but I didn't say anything. I couldn't trust her. She said she was going to lay down and rest. I got up and left her room. I was amazed that she didn't punish me. Maybe she was beginning to understand our plight. Or maybe she simply didn't have the strength and energy to exact her revenge on me.

The next day came. We got up and all got ready, each one taking a turn in the bathroom. We came downstairs to see Timmy sitting there and eating some food with Mom. I wouldn't say he seemed happy but he seemed calm. I guessed that they had spoken and she had let him come back upstairs after being satisfied that he had learned his lesson. I think by now my mother was recovering as the stab wounds clearly weren't life-threatening. She was back to her loud domineering self and was at the helm once again. It's like what happened had suddenly been forgotten. We were so surprised to see Timmy and to see him eating with my mom calmly sitting in the seat near him. She was watching a programme called 'The Ricki Lake Show.' They weren't talking but all seemed very calm in the living room. We were all feeling hungry so Sally decided she would make breakfast for her, Lizzy and myself. The day went by quickly and there were no events to speak of. But I wasn't convinced that things had changed. I had made that mistake before so I didn't plan on doing that again. I kept my cards close to my chest and kept one eye on my mother at all times. She had become somewhat unpredictable and I didn't want to take any chances.

Chapter 7

By this point, my mother had completely recovered from her wounds. She was back to her usual, shouting and insulting us. Sometimes the loudest person in the room has the most to hide. Nothing had changed and I knew that would be the case because a leopard never changes its spots. In the next few days, the most shocking thing was to happen and I will reveal all. My mother had become very wary of me. She would keep her eyes on us all the time, more so than usual. Staring at us as we walked past her, she would almost be startled and heed our presence in a way she hadn't done before. Any time she didn't know where we were in the house, she would shout out and demand that we come and see her. She did this a lot from that point onwards. She didn't trust us. She would also lie a lot more. I could tell. For example, she would say she was going out but then return after five minutes and pretend that she forgot something. She would tell us dinner was ready and then change her mind. She was acting strangely, to say the least. What I learned as I got older is that if someone lies to you, the more likely it is that they need something from you. It always felt like my mom wanted something from me when she lied to me. I knew when she was lying too.

Timmy seemed a bit better and he was a bit more talkative. Lizzy was her usual bashful self and Sally was always inquisitive. Me, on the other hand, I was just unsure what to do with myself. I knew things were awkward between my mother and me. She looked at me every time with contempt and a suspicious eye.

On this particular day, we were all at home just doing mundane things and lounging around the house. My mother had got me a Walkman and I had put some music on it. My favourites were RnB and slow jams. I was just laying on my bed listening to some music, chilling. It was around 3 pm and we had all just eaten. Things seemed placid in the house and my mother was on the sofa watching her tv programmes. That's the thing when she was home, she would never let us have free reign over the tv. It was always what she wanted to watch. You would think that parents would let their kids watch some tv during the day and then watch tv at night time when they were asleep. Maybe she didn't want us getting brainwashed by television and media. But she was brainwashing us anyway in terms of how she raised us. It was all a system of control.

I was enjoying my time in isolation. It was nice to be away from everyone and just in my own world and listening to some good music. Music is like a message frozen in time. It's timeless and it opens up something in you that brings life and joy to you. I loved music and it was the one thing my mother got for me that I appreciated because she didn't get us many things over the years. She was niggardly. But it complimented her personality and attitude towards us. I heard the door to my bedroom squeak and then open – Sally came into the room and asked me what I was up to. I removed one earphone from my ear to hear what she was saying and I just told her that I was chilling and listening to music. She seemed to have a lot on her mind. I asked her what was up and she just shrugged her shoulders as if to say she didn't know, but that didn't mean nothing was up. I wasn't sure what she was trying to say. She looked at me with an intense gaze and told me that she noticed some blood coming out of her private part. I had already gone through this stage and it was my mother who taught me a bit about it. We kept sanitary towels in the bathroom for all of us to use. I explained the whole cycle to Sally and she seemed to understand. The puzzled look on her face dissipated. She and I spent the rest of the day in our room just talking about life and our plans for when we grew up. Sally said that when she left the house she wanted to get married and be someone that works with children in need. I found that to be laudable. That was very nice of her to say. I had no idea what I wanted to do with my life, but I could only think as far as my nose. I wanted to just be away from my mother, that much I knew. One day, I said, one day.

The next day I woke up early – I had to make breakfast for everyone. I got up and headed to the bathroom. I picked up my pink toothbrush and put toothpaste on it. I started brushing my teeth. While I was brushing my teeth, I heard a knock on the door. My mother was there – I could tell by the heaviness of the way she gripped the handle. She tried to open it but I had locked the door. She asked who was inside the bathroom and, at first, I didn't respond. She asked again and I just admitted that it was me and that I would soon be done. I could detect a hint of frustration in her voice when she said, "Okay." I spent about two more minutes in the bathroom. I finally got out and my mother quickly came to the door, brushed past me as she did and went in there. She huffed and slammed the door behind her. She had never needed the bathroom that urgently before but I suppose she needed to use the loo or something. She was in there for a good ten minutes. I went back to my room to put on my robe and then I headed downstairs to cook breakfast. I was going to make pancakes and syrup for everyone. I know Timmy and Lizzy loved my pancakes. I got to the kitchen and took out all of the crockery and cutlery I needed to make the mixture. I got two eggs, some milk, flour, sugar and cinnamon and blended it all together. I dipped my finger in the mixture to taste to see if it was right. It tasted lovely. I then put on the stove and started frying the pancakes one by one. I couldn't wait – I ate two before I had finished making them. They were delicious. About 30 minutes later, I called everyone to come and get their food. I also added strawberries to the breakfast. My mother seemed very pleased with my efforts and thanked me for making the food. We all sat at the dinner table and indulged in the food. I could see Timmy stuffing his face. Some syrup was even dripping down his chin as he tried to lick it, and when that failed, he cleaned it off with his hand. He was like a voracious animal. Everyone commented on how tasty the pancakes were, so I was rather pleased with myself. It was quiet around the table as it often was, but I was just happy that everyone was eating my food. It seemed like it was a calm day but no one could foresee what was about to come.

My next duty was to do the laundry that day. I got up and picked up everyone's plate from the dinner table. Everyone thanked me. I put the dirty dishes in the sink. It was full to the brim with dishes. Sally had dishes duty that day. I went upstairs to the bathroom and picked up the dirty clothes basket and carried it down with me to the basement. It felt like it weighed a ton. It felt weird being down there again because of years before when my mother had left me down there for months. It was like a phantom to me that I couldn't get rid of. I still occasionally suffer from sleepless nights because of what happened to me. I wasn't sure what my mother thought of me anymore because I had tried unsuccessfully to kill her twice. She had now fully recovered from her stab wounds. I still couldn't believe I had done that. Little old me had the gall to try and kill her but I felt like I didn't have a choice under the circumstances. Things weren't conventional in my house. You wouldn't think that my mother would stay in the same house with someone who had tried to kill her, but she was so determined to have us stay with her no matter what and so we did. I was in the basement sorting out the clothes. I was going to do two wash cycles, whites and colours. I turned on the washing machine and arranged all the whites that I wanted to put on. Some of the clothing items were filthy, particularly Timmy's stuff. I put them in the washing machine and set them for a long wash at 60 degrees. I stayed down there for a bit, alone with my thoughts. The washing was far into its cycle. Without realising, I had been down there for about forty-five minutes. I didn't feel like going upstairs anyway. It was best that I stayed away from my mother as much as I could. I didn't trust her and she didn't trust me. Every time I was around her, it felt like there was an elephant in the room.

The clothes had finished washing. I took them out and put the colours in. The machine was rather old so it would make a ringing sound as it spun around. I went upstairs and I asked for my mom's permission to hang them up on the line in the backyard. She consented. I walked back downstairs, went outside to the backyard, and started hanging up the whites individually. It was tedious as we had a lot of clothes between five people. I got it done and just sat on the porch for five minutes. Surprisingly, my mother didn't come outside to berate me for doing that. I came back inside and just sat on the dying sofa which had abrasion marks from all the times we had sat on it. My mother was very quiet and hadn't engaged much with us that day. She just left us to our own devices. Even in our teens, Sally and I never had cell phones. We didn't have friends anyway, so who would we be talking to? I always wanted a cell phone. My mother had one. But never got us one. I was sitting watching tv with my mother, Sally and Lizzy. Timmy was upstairs in his room. I had no idea what he was doing. Being the only boy, he would often do that and just sit on his own and do his own thing. He didn't want to always be around us women. It was time to get up and check on the washing – so I did just that. I felt a bit lazy but I didn't want my mother to see me lazing around the house. I summoned up the energy to get myself off the sofa and headed downstairs, but I almost fell over as I did. The clothes had finished washing and it was time to take them outside and hang them up on a separate washing line. It didn't take me long as there weren't that many clothes in the bunch. I finished doing that and headed back inside. I remember asking my mother if it was going to rain that day. She quickly went to the news channel and checked the weather forecast. No rain. I sat down and just twiddled my thumbs and disappeared into the sofa.

Sometime later, I was woken up by a screaming match between my mother and Sally. Lizzy seemed so demure and unnerved by the argument. I wasn't sure what it was about but Sally was being accused of lying and she was defending herself. I was so confused. I didn't know what to do, so I just stayed out of it. My mother was seething. She was in a rage. I had seen that kind of rage in her eyes many a time and knew you couldn't placate her. Her face was bright red and she was slurring her words such was her anger. They carried on exchanging words and she stood up and stormed towards Sally. She punched her dead in the face and Sally recoiled. Her head tilted back and she held her left cheek. When she recovered and put her face up, my mother hit her again. It's like she was a boxer. Sally tried to defend herself by just holding her body in a submissive and apologetic manner. But it didn't stop my mother from carrying on. She grabbed Sally by the arm and hauled her across the room. Sally just stood there defencelessly and started to cry. Timmy had emerged from his lair at the top of the stairs to see what was going on. He had a puzzled look on his face – he wore a frown and a slight grimace. He pleaded with my mother to stop but she didn't relent. She carried on slapping Sally around the face and kicked her twice in the stomach. Sally fell back and ended up on the floor. My mother was in a rage; at this point, it was like she saw red. Nothing could stop her. Lizzy and I were also pleading with her to stop beating Sally. Then suddenly, my mom put her hands around Sally's neck. She started to strangle her. Sally was trying her best to get some words out but they slowly faded away. She was going blue in the face as Lizzy and I stood behind my mother unable to do anything to help. She just kept strangling her and slamming her head on the wooden floor. It seemed to go on for an age and all of a sudden Sally had stopped moving, but my mother didn't stop, she just kept at it. She was rag-dolling her head with so much anger and contempt. She finally stopped her attack and released Sally. We all gasped and were shocked into a state of stupor. Sally lay there motionless and I knew something bad had happened. I had never seen someone that limp before so I knew something was really wrong. Lizzy and I started calling Sally's name. My mother got up and went to the kitchen to smoke a cigarette. She often did that after beating us. Maybe it calmed her nerves, I don't know. I headed over to Sally and tried to shake her to wake up. "Wake up!" I said, "Wake up." She didn't respond. I didn't know about a pulse or anything at that age, but all I knew was that she wasn't moving at all. My mother came back to the living room and asked us to move away. So we did. She gently touched Sally's shoulder and tried to shrug her a bit while we watched attentively, hoping she would get up. Nothing worked. My mother started saying, "Oh, my God. What have I done?" She seemed to show some remorse for her actions. Judging by her reaction, I could tell that Sally had perished; she was DEAD. My mother was trying to feel Sally's neck and her wrists. I wasn't sure what she was doing but now I realise she was trying to feel for a pulse. I then suggested that we call the ambulance. "We have to call the ambulance now!" I said, but my mother told me not to. I fell back into my seat and I was in complete shock. I then remembered that news footage that I watched of that little girl whose mother had killed her. Thoughts were racing around in my head, crashing into each other as they did. I never thought it would be one of my siblings; I always thought it would be me to die. We left Sally in that position, but I did go upstairs to get a duvet from her bed to cover her. I touched her and she was cold to the touch. Frozen. You couldn't move her even if you were Superman. I now know she was in the rigor mortis phase. She was deceased. I just couldn't believe what had happened. Mother told us to all go to our rooms and so we did with our heads down, saddened and afraid. Timmy still didn't know what had happened. He shut himself in his room in fear when he heard what was happening. I didn't want to tell him either. He would be broken. He loved us all very much, and even though we sometimes argued, I know he adored us. He was also very protective.

Some time passed. Lizzy was in my room with me and Timmy was in his room. He knocked on my door and I jumped up to answer because I was half-expecting it to be my mother with some good news. It was him. I let him in and he had a concerned look on his face. He wondered why we were all in my room. I had to break the news to him. I told him that something bad had happened. Sally was dead. I saw his facial expression change immediately. It was a mix between anger and sadness. A tear fell down his cheek at first – he was holding his head in his hands. He then burst into tears and just kept asking, "Why? What happened? Why didn't you do more to stop Mother?" I had no answers for him, just disappointment and sadness in my eyes. I was crestfallen. We all just sat there crying and hugging each other. I told them that everything would be okay and that we had to be strong for each other. I could hear my mother pacing up and down downstairs too – anxious and talking to herself. She climbed the stairs and I could hear her approaching. About halfway up, she called me and told me to come downstairs. I emerged from my prison cell and followed her and asked her if she was going to report what had happened. She said no because she wouldn't be allowed to take care of us anymore. 'Good,' I thought. She had told me that we had to go and put Sally to rest far away. She told me that on that night, we would get up and drive Sally across the country and leave her somewhere. I could tell it was going to be a long trip because my mother started preparing some food to leave for Timmy and Lizzy, I assumed. Lizzy was 10, so she would have to babysit Timmy, as big as he was. My mother instructed me to help her lift up Sally's body and put it in the trunk of her car. She was so stiff. It felt so weird picking her up. I wanted to throw up and I couldn't look her in the face. It broke my heart. Was I an accomplice now? We lifted her dead weight and put her in the trunk of the car – she felt so heavy. I couldn't believe my little sister was gone. I had to control my emotions. I couldn't break down in front of my mother but I just couldn't help it. She kept telling me to stop crying and to wipe the tears from my face. So I did. I tried. I started having flashbacks of Sally as a little girl and us being inseparable. I was devastated. She told me to sit in the front passenger seat whilst she went inside to get something. I assumed she had told Lizzy to look after Timmy and that there was plenty of food for them to eat, etc. She came back in a hurry and sat down next to me in the car. I was beside myself; I couldn't believe what was happening. But I was just a passenger. She started the car and we headed off. I don't think she even knew exactly where she was going. But it was obvious that she wanted to get as far away as possible. We got to the highway and I saw signage for Highway 51. We got on it and just started driving. Just driving and driving. Hours had passed and I had fallen asleep. I had no inkling as to where we were. My mother had stopped the car at a gas station to fill up the tank and get some water. She got back in the car and we carried on. I saw signs and I think we were now in Houston. We turned towards San Antonio and we got onto the interstate 35 North. We carried on for hours and hours. It was now about 4 in the morning. Still very dark outside. We ended up in a place called Pearsall. This was as far outside of my house as I had ever gone in my 13 years of life. It looked so different. So many buildings; so many woods too. I hadn't forgotten why we were there. Throughout the journey, my mother hardly said a word to me. She suddenly turned off the road into a kind of secluded area in the woods. It was dark and eerie but at least we were in a car. We drove into it for about 2 minutes and then my mother stopped the car. She ordered me to get out and come to the trunk of the car. I obliged. She had a shovel in the trunk and she picked it up and started digging while I just watched her. It felt like it was a movie. It really did. She was digging and digging until she was satisfied. She asked me to help her pick up the body and put it in the grave. I grabbed Sally's feet and my mother grabbed her head. We lifted her and placed her in the grave. I stepped back and my mother started filling it up. I started tearing up again as I realised that was the last time I would ever see my little sister. My mother had finished filling up the hole and put the shovel back in the trunk. She used her feet to kick away some tyre tracks near the scene; I didn't understand why. We got back in the car and made the long journey back home. I was so afraid that it would be one of us next on my mother's list. She just snapped and killed Sally.

It seemed to get light very quickly after we left Sally's body. I fell asleep again and was awoken by the ray of the sun's light shining through the windscreen and onto my face. The signs were still saying more than a hundred miles to Raymond, Mississippi. I just stared out of the window and mourned my sister's death. I couldn't believe I was going back to the same house as this killer, but was I any better? We got back and my mother quickly went into the kitchen to get some detergent and cloths to clean her trunk. She started cleaning her trunk out and told me to go back inside, so I did. I saw Lizzy and Timmy and I immediately hugged them and we all started crying and I kept saying, "Sorry, Sally." In my mind, however, at least she was free from all the suffering. In a better place in heaven. My mother spent at least an hour in the garage cleaning everything up. She came back inside and had a look on her face like someone was chasing her. For the rest of the day, the household was quiet. No one hardly said a word to each other. We were all just sad that Sally was gone and gone for good. It was surreal. Later that evening, when I went into my room, I looked over at Sally's bed. I saw all of her clothing and her little toy collection and Barbies and I just felt a huge sad feeling in my heart. I cried and cried. Somehow, I even blamed myself for what had happened to her. I felt like I could have done more to protect her but I froze when it mattered. I had already tried to murder my mother before, so why couldn't I have jumped in when she was strangling Sally? That lived with me and it still does to this day. I stayed up all night clinging to my pillow for solace. I was so lonely. I missed Sally's presence and just being able to talk to her during the night. We hadn't even started discussing female issues like boyfriends and things like that. What a shame she was gone. With every minute that passed, I grew sadder. I felt so down and I started feeling nauseous. I didn't know what to do with myself. I started to feel tired but I couldn't bring myself to fall asleep. It just didn't sit right with me, her being gone and me being back here. This was inevitable and my mother was trying to get away with the murder of my little sister. For the next few weeks, the house was just quiet. My mother would occasionally have an outburst but she was generally very calm. We were all feeling the loss of Sally. It was unchartered territory for us all. It made us grow closer.

Chapter 8

It was a quiet Sunday afternoon. We were all still reeling from the loss of Sally. We were all sitting at the dinner table and my mother was cooking dinner for one less person. It just felt so alien to not have Sally there with us. The room felt bigger and emptier than it usually did. We sat and ate in silence, just lost and aloof from each other. It stayed like that for months and months. We had to live with her loss and couldn't even mourn her properly.

Years had passed and I was 17, Lizzy was 14 and Timmy was 12. Sally would have been 16. No one ever came to our house to inquire about her death. I was so surprised. It seemed that my mother had gotten away with it, or so she thought. I had seen a lot of tv shows where people are eventually caught for committing murders but it had seemed that my mother had gotten away with it up to this point. None of us was brave enough to call the police on her, because we knew that it would take time to convict someone, and by then, my mother would have gotten hold of us. On this particular day, apparently, my mother had called someone to come and do some landscaping in the back garden. Maybe because she was getting older, she had started to care about things like that. All I knew was that we would have to avoid interacting with whoever came to the house. So, I wasn't interested. It went without saying. My mother walked about halfway up the staircase and shouted out that a man was coming to do the gardening and that we should be on our best behaviour. I acknowledged her and just carried on sitting in my room. As I got older, my mother was less strict about us being on our own. She left us to our own devices, and naturally, as you get older, you start to spend more time on your own, as you become yourself. I know if Sally had been here, she and I would always have been together. I was starting to worry about Timmy and Lizzy; they were getting older too and both had very different personalities. I always tried to protect them in any way that I could. Timmy and Lizzy shared a room. It was only when he was young that he slept in my mother's room. My mother did say that she thought it would be a good idea if Lizzy came to my room, to take Sally's bed and that Timmy could have that room to himself because he was a boy and needed his space and privacy. But it was yet to happen. I heard the doorbell ring and I immediately tensed up – my mother quickly answered it. She opened the door and I could hear her speaking to a man. It was the landscaper. About five minutes later, I could hear a lot of movement in the back garden. I was a bit curious. I expected to see some old man with his little rake and gardener hat in the back garden. I got up and walked over to the window to see what was going on. I was surprised at what I saw. Jeez! A young, tall, dark-haired virile man. He was muscular in build. He had a chiselled jaw and had a gaunt face. He was wearing a tank top and a blue overall. He had a hat on but had long hair streaming down the sides of his face. He was the first man I'd seen in the flesh for years but he was gorgeous. I had seen a lot of men on tv who I found attractive but this man had me blushing. I couldn't take my eyes off him. I just watched him and watched him work on the garden which he made look so effortless and graceful. Lizzy came to my room and I immediately got startled. I quickly ran back to my bed and tried to pretend as if I wasn't looking at anything from the window. She had caught me, however. She walked over to the window and saw the landscaper in all his glory and looked at me and gave me a mirthful smile. I said, "What?" trying to feign innocence. I had a smile on my face and it stayed on my face throughout the day. I needed an external stimulant, something different, something I could look forward to. if I had to guess, I would have said he was about 22 or maybe 23. Definitely older than me but still young enough to have caught my eye. I asked Lizzy what she wanted and she gave me the puppy dog eyes then asked to borrow my Walkman, so I gave it to her. She quickly left the room, but not soon enough so I could go back to ogling at this gorgeous man. I went back to the window and he was still busy with his work. He was beautiful. I noticed myself playing with my hair as I just kept my eyes firmly on him. I could have watched him all day. I was standing there just long enough I think for him to feel eyes on him. He turned his head and looked upstairs and saw me. I ducked down as quickly as I could but I was mortified. "Oh, my God, did he see me?" I wondered. I was so embarrassed but then I smiled to myself. Maybe I wanted him to know that I had noticed him. Who wouldn't? I slowly moved my head back up and peered over the ledge to see if he was still looking – he wasn't. Some time had passed and I could hear my mother's voice coming from the back garden – she was loud and coarse. Her voice was echoing so loudly that it was like she was showing off or wanted to be the centre of attention. I crawled to the window and peeped to see what was going on. My mother was talking to this man and it was so obvious that she was flirting with him, flinging her hair back and forth, twirling around, laughing at everything he said. She had on a skirt and a spaghetti-string top. I was furious that a woman her age would even entertain a man his age. My dreams were dashed. I couldn't compete. About an hour later, my mother came to my room and said she was popping out quickly. I got excited because I knew it was my opportunity to talk to him and get him to notice me. I had never used makeup before but I had seen adverts on tv about it and had an idea on how to apply it. This is exactly what I needed Sally for. My mother left and I ran to her room, found her make-up bag, emptied the contents of it onto her dresser, found what I wanted and started applying some lipstick and foundation. I didn't want to overdo it, but I was happy with how I looked I looked in the mirror one last time pursed my lips and smiled to myself. I put everything back in its place and walked back to my room to put on my favourite red dress and I had some slippers on. I had to make sure I did all this before my mother came back home. I had to move quickly. I walked downstairs; I was nervous but excited. I couldn't wait to see him up close. I opened the sliding doors and walked up to him – his back was to me at the time. I was so nervous that my left leg started to shake as I approached him. He was crouched down working on a particular section of the garden. I think he was removing the roots or something. "Hi," I said. It startled him. He jumped when I said it. He then turned around and flashed the most perfect smile at me after gathering himself. My heart melted. I was in love. "Oh, hey!" he said. I then asked him if I could get him anything like water or a hot drink and he said no. We got into a conversation but I noticed how inexperienced I was in life, so I was very laconic with my answers. But somehow, he seemed to be intrigued by me too. I was smiling at him non-stop and it was written all over my face that I was infatuated with him. My smile was wide and it was stuck on my face – my eyes were lit and I loved the way his voice changed when he would talk about something he was excited about. A lot of the conversation was about him and his job. I was fascinated. He could have been talking about anything and I still would have been interested. He eventually called me 'beautiful' and 'winsome.' I had never had these sorts of feelings before and I was loving it. It was something different, something positive. There was hardly anything positive to look forward to in my life so I was relishing this. We laughed and laughed and I got lost in time. I realised that my mother would probably be back at any minute and told him that I had to go. I didn't want to. He understood and said it had been a pleasure meeting me. He said he would be back the following day to complete his work. I smiled and kept my eyes on him, then I turned around and ran back inside. I rushed back almost falling over as I did. I went to the bathroom and washed the makeup off my face – I just stared in the mirror looked at my reflection and smiled to myself. I then went to my room, took off the red dress and just put on some house clothes, then I stayed in my room and laid on my bed staring at the ceiling thinking about him. I felt so happy. I couldn't wait to see him again.

My mother got back and as usual, she was up to her flirtatious antics. She was acting desperate as far as I was concerned. He was being polite and nice to her but I didn't believe he was genuinely interested in her. Before I left him, I made sure to tell him not to mention that we had spoken and he promised not to tell, so, I thought I was safe. Another hour or so passed and I looked out of the window again and saw him packing up his things. It felt like my heart was breaking because I was so anxious that I wouldn't see him again. If I did, what would I say to him? Would he still be interested in me?

The next day came and I heard a knock on the door. I jumped out of bed – hair messy, sleep in my eyes, bad breath, and I ran to answer the door. He had returned to the house bright and early. My mother was upstairs in her room and was too slow to answer the door. I was up early and about to carry out my kitchen duties. We gave each other a warm smile at the door. I called out to my mother who quickly came downstairs to greet him. She almost pushed me out of the way when she arrived at the door. She led him to the garden and he carried on with the work he had started the previous day. Lizzy and Timmy were in the living room watching tv whilst my mother was outside trying her hardest to impress him. She seemed so randy in the way she was talking to him. I was watching their every move. Every now and again, I would peer through the sliding doors and have a look at them together. She eventually pried herself away from the garden and came back inside. She shouted at me for not doing the dishes quicker and I said nothing. It was like she was trying to assert herself as the dominant woman in the household. Luckily, I don't think that he heard the exchange between us. I didn't want him to know what my mother was like with me. I feared that this would make me look unattractive in his eyes. I was still so excited about him being around. The fact it seemed like he found me attractive made me so happy, even though I was starting to look more like my mom every day. I wanted to ask him a million questions and get to know him better, but I didn't know how it would work. Maybe if things worked out, he could come over late at night and we could sit in his van, talk and get to know each other. I just imagined so many different types of scenarios in my mind. My mother went upstairs to the bathroom and I took the opportunity to quickly go and see him. When I got to the door, I realised how beautiful he was. He looked even better that day than he had the day before. I had to act quickly. I made a sort of bird noise to get his attention; he then turned and I smiled at him and gestured to him to be quiet. I went up to him and hugged him and I felt so many emotions rushing through my body. It felt amazing. I whispered to him that I wanted to see him again. He said, "When?" I explained that he could come over the next day late at night and that I would meet him outside. He smiled and said, "What time?" I told him at around midnight. He agreed and I quickly retreated back to the kitchen, careful not to give myself away, and carried on with the dishes and cleaning.

I was so excited about seeing him the next day. I couldn't wait. I had butterflies in my stomach. He just seemed so calm and collected. He seemed attentive and sweet but this was my first ever romantic crush on someone, so I had to be careful. My mother got out of the shower and seemed in good spirits. I could hear her humming to herself. Evil b**ch. You killed your own daughter – how can you be okay and be humming? I was sitting in the living room with Timmy and Lizzy. Lizzy was talking to me and every so often she would tease me about my new crush. I would angrily admonish her and then she would stop. My mother came downstairs and headed straight out to the back garden. I felt jealous. She had the opportunity to engage with him again. I was so curious to know what exactly she was saying to him but I didn't want to make it obvious. But I kept looking over toward the back garden – anxious and curious. She spent a good ten minutes outside with him and I couldn't hear what they were saying because she had closed the sliding doors behind her. Soon after, they both emerged in the living room, chatting and laughing away at each other's jokes. They were so jocular and merry. It hurt me to see him talk to another woman in that way, especially her. He came into the house and said goodbye to all of us. We acknowledged him. I pretended to be uninterested but he gave me a cheeky little wink before he set off. He left and I was so excited about seeing him the next night. We had a date.

The next day came and I was constantly thinking about how I would dress up for him, what I would wear, and what I would say. To be honest, I was just happy to spend some time with him outside of the house. I always saw these women on tv with tons of makeup and the skimpiest dresses on to lure men. I had kind of hoped he wouldn't see me differently without makeup on. I couldn't put any on seeing as it was all in my mother's room. The day went by fast and I grew more nervous the closer it got to bedtime. I told my mother I was going to sleep early at around 9 pm whilst Timmy, Mom and Lizzy were all still downstairs. I wasn't going to sleep at all. I was just going to visualise my perfect date with this man. I didn't even know his name at that point. About an hour passed and I could hear Timmy and Lizzy lazily passing my door and going to their room. Soon after, my mother also headed to bed. I was listening out for any peculiar noises. I had to make sure everyone was sound asleep before I got up to see him. It was 23:45 and I was so excited. I opened my door a bit and I could hear my mother snoring. She was fast asleep. I snuck into the bathroom and washed my face and fixed my hair. I took it out of the bun it was in and just straightened it as much as I could. I turned off the light and headed back to my room. I found a nice yellow dress that my mother had bought for me when I was 16. It was a tight fit and showed off my legs. I wanted him to like me for who I was, not what I had or how I looked. Wearing that dress was a test, I guess. I snuck downstairs, careful to avoid the parts of the wooden floor on the landing that creaked. I headed downstairs as quietly as a mouse. I peeked out of the front window and saw his red truck outside. My heart was in my mouth, but I was excited, I have to admit. I got to the front door and as the key was in the door, I unlocked it and walked outside, tiptoeing as I did. I closed the door gently, took the keys and locked it behind me. I saw that big smile on his face that I recognised so well. I gave him a nervous smile back. I got to his car; I think it was a Chevy. He jumped out and walked over to my side to open the door for me; so gallant. Just before I sat down, he gave me a warm embrace. He smelled so good; I didn't want to let him go. I had to be careful because my mother's room was on the other side of the house which was in full view of the driveway. When I got into the car, it smelled like aftershave and cigarettes. He walked around the car and jumped in. He asked me if I was okay and I said I was. I told him to drive somewhere nearby where we could sit and talk. So he did. He drove to some creek about two minutes from my house. I was nervous for the whole drive. I then realised I could have been in danger. I didn't know who this man was. But I wanted to take the risk as I was so attracted to him. He spoke in a soft but sonorous manly voice. He had brown eyes and dark long hair. He had a bit of stubble which I loved. I kept my eyes on him and couldn't look away. We started talking and I asked him his name. He told me his name was Tony. I told him mine and he said it was beautiful just like I was. I was grinning from ear to ear. I couldn't help it. He was stimulating so many positive emotions in me with his conversation and comments. He gave me his full attention and was challenging as a man should be. I was falling for him even more. He kept biting his lip and that was so attractive to me. He was also extremely confident. One thing I noticed that he did was he kept pulling and pushing me emotionally and mentally. It made me super attracted to him. I could tell he knew how to treat women and had a lot of experience, but I didn't let that get in the way.

We were talking for about an hour I'd say. I found out a lot about him. He was 22 indeed, he had no kids, was a landscaper and had his own apartment in Raymond. He went to school close to where I lived. I told him I was home-schooled but never explained why. He didn't ask, he just let me talk and be myself. I told him about my family but lied about how great our life was. I even told him that I had lost my sister and that she was killed in a car crash when she was 15. He hugged me and told me that things would be okay; he was so sweet. I couldn't tell him the truth. He said he was a Taurus. He suddenly said something which almost threw me. He said, "We are going to be such good friends." My heart dropped and I felt rejected. I sat there with my arms folded and had a puzzled look on my face. He laughed and just said he was joking, which put a smile on my face. We just had a moment where we were both staring into each other's eyes and it was like magic. The connection we felt. I could have stayed with him all night. He was a complete gentleman but also a bit cheeky and edgy and I loved that. I told him that I needed to head back home before my mom woke up and realised I wasn't home. He started the car and we headed back. Just as we got back, I smiled at him and thanked him for a lovely evening. He smiled back and asked when he could see me again. I said I didn't have a phone but I would love to see him again the following day at the same time. We agreed. Just at that moment, I wanted to kiss him. Who am I kidding? I had wanted to kiss him from the moment I saw him. We embraced and we touched lips. It was so amazing and electric. I had never felt such emotion and sensations coursing through my body. It was the best thing ever and he tasted so sweet. We kissed for about a minute. I was inexperienced but he led me with his experience and I just followed. I opened the car door and hesitated to leave. I finally got out of the car and I walked towards my front door turning my head and staring at him whilst I did. We just kept a fixed smile on our faces. I got to the front door and took my keys out. They were jangling a bit but I was quiet enough. He kept his engine running and he drove off. I opened the door and went inside. I closed the door behind me and just stood there with my back against the door and gently caressed my lips. I was so happy. I wanted to see him again and again. I snuck up to my room and could still hear my mom snoring which gave me comfort. I got into my bed, and at that moment, I remembered Sally. It's a shame she wasn't there for me to share this experience with. She was my best friend. I felt sad for a while. I eventually fell asleep and woke up nice and early the next day with a big smile on my face. I was going to see him again. My mother was in a foul mood. She was shouting at me about everything. It got so bad that she slapped me for not taking out the garbage bin. I held my face and just remembered how bad my life really was. The night before was like a fairy tale, but reality hit back. I just tried to forget about my mother and focus on the night that lay ahead.

It got to about 10 pm and again I said I was heading to bed. My mother just snarled at me but I didn't react to her. Timmy and Lizzy were already in bed sleeping. My mother stayed downstairs a bit longer this time and I grew anxious. I was meant to meet Tony at midnight and it was approaching 11 pm. I had no way of communicating with him and changing the time. I still took the risk and was going to see him no matter what. At about 11:30 pm, I heard my mother heading upstairs. I knew she wouldn't be asleep by midnight but I was planning on being ultra-quiet and stealthy. I didn't want to get caught. I snuck out as soon as he arrived. I waited in the living room for a minute to see if my mother would come back downstairs and she didn't. I got into his car and this time he drove to the end of the road. I was worried that she would see his headlights pulling up to the driveway, but her curtains were drawn when I looked up behind me. We had the best night ever. He told me he wanted me to be with him and that if things went well, we could get married and have children. Yes, I was scared but I felt so strongly for him. I couldn't hide the feelings I had. What he said didn't scare me off. It attracted me to him even more. I spent about three hours with him and at around 3 am, he started the car. I decided this time to walk back to my house to avoid him pulling up there again. It was scary but I was so happy that I didn't even notice anything strange as I walked.

For the next two months, I saw him almost every night. We built a strong bond and we eventually had intercourse in the back of his truck. It was amazing and I think I fell in love with him as soon as it happened. We started planning to live together but he still didn't know anything about how evil my mother was. We would laugh and laugh and just have such a good time together. Once we even went for a drive and another time went to the lake and just parked there and talked for hours. I started seeing him later and later, just to ensure my mother was asleep. I was tired but I always slept well after seeing him. I never got caught which was the biggest surprise of all. My mother had no idea of what I was doing. She was still a nightmare and she had recently beaten Lizzy with a belt because she didn't do her schoolwork correctly. But this was my out, my way of being in a different world. Tony made me feel like anything was possible and that I wasn't in prison anymore, or at least, wouldn't be forever.

One day, I realised that I had to tell my mother what was going on. I noticed that my period hadn't come. But I also wanted to tell her that I intended on moving out and living with Tony. It was for two reasons: One, to get away from her, and two, to be with Tony. I had to tell her, but I had to find the right moment. I decided I was going to tell her one Saturday afternoon. In front of my siblings too. I was sitting in the living room with her and my siblings. We had just eaten lunch and were lounging on the sofas. Timmy let out a huge belch as he rubbed his stomach. It made Lizzy and I laugh. I called my mother to the kitchen and told her I had something to say. She listened attentively as I broke the news to her. I never told her that I thought I might be pregnant. That would have been too much for her to handle, I thought. I told her that I had met someone and that I really liked him and was considering moving in with him. She immediately laughed at me and asked who it was. She then said, "You don't go anywhere; how did you meet someone?" I paused and knew she wouldn't approve of Tony seeing as she was flirting with him herself. I explained that it was the landscaper and she almost dropped to the floor in disbelief. She asked me when I had even spoken to him. She then asked why I was so mendacious and I didn't know what to say. I told her I was going to move out in a few weeks and she wasn't happy. Still, I was going to leave the house if it killed me. Timmy and Lizzy were old enough to take care of themselves at that point, so I didn't feel that bad about it. We argued about it and she told me that I was never to see him again. I stood there defiantly and thought about it. I would have to run away. It wouldn't be difficult. I decided that I didn't want to leave like that.

I wanted to leave of my own volition and in my own time. I didn't want to sneak out, never to be seen again. I waited and waited. I still snuck out to see Tony over the next few weeks. I didn't want to poke the beast, so to speak.

The day came when I was planning on moving out. Tony was going to pick me up in the evening. My mother was aware as I had told her but she repudiated it. I knew we may get into a physical altercation because of it but I didn't care. It got to the evening and Tony was meant to be arriving at around 8 pm. I had already packed all my things and I was ready. I went to Lizzy and Timmy's room and I told them how much I loved them. I told them that I would come and check on them and that I wasn't far away. I explained that I was older now and that it was time for me to move on. Lizzy giggled but looked sad and she asked me if it was the man who did the garden. My smile gave it away, so I just said yes. She could see how in love I was. I gave them both the longest and the biggest hug I could and I told Timmy that Mom would probably let him have mine and Sally's old room. He was just sad. They both asked me not to leave, but I promised them I would be back to check on them from time to time. Yes, I did feel bad about leaving but I had to do this for myself. My whole life I had tried to protect them and it was time for me to move on. I was worried about them and about how they would cope alone with my mother but there was nothing I could do. I left their room and when I got to the door, I turned back one more time and said goodbye to them. I had a tear in my eye; I felt sad. I closed the door behind me and just paused there for a few seconds, composed myself and went into my room. I started gathering all of my things. It wasn't that much. Just two suitcases full of clothes, toiletries, etc., and one or two things of Sally's. I snuck into my mother's room, looked out the window whilst she was downstairs and saw that Tony was already waiting for me in the driveway. I had already told him that it was best that he didn't come inside to help out. That would have just been awkward. I went back to my room and grabbed the first suitcase. I took it downstairs and walked right past my mother who just huffed as I did. I went to his truck and put it in there and came back inside. I headed past her again and went to my room to grab the second suitcase. When I came back downstairs, she was on her feet. She was clamouring and asking me what I was doing. I told her we had been through this and that I was leaving. She said, "You don't even know him!" I explained that I did and that I loved him. She grabbed hold of me and I thought, 'No more!' I pushed her hands away. I told her if she harmed my siblings, she would be sorry. I also told her that I would come and visit Timmy and Lizzy and she told me not to bother, but I didn't care. I already knew that I would come and see them. I planned to get them cell phones when I found a bit of money so that I could communicate with them. They would have to hide them away from my mother though, because if she found out, she would punish them and confiscate the phones. I barged past her with my last suitcase and when I got to the door, I looked back at her and told her she had failed as a mother. She gave me a look full of disdain and said, "Whatever". She then said I better not tell him about her and what she had done. I nodded in agreement because at that moment I felt a bit scared of her again. I then just turned around, opened the door and took the short walk to freedom. I felt so powerful at that moment. My mom briefly came to the door to look out, but when she saw me, she slammed the door shut. I got into the car and just told Tony to drive. We got to this small, old-looking house that he was apparently renting. Tony told me to wait at the door while he got my suitcases. He came back and I heard the jangle of his keys. He opened the door and I felt like I was in heaven. The property was beautifully decorated. It had three bedrooms and a big bathroom, a big living room and a prodigious backyard. I was so happy I could start the next chapter in my life. I gave him a big hug and kiss and we embraced for about two minutes on the sofa. I was home; I was free.

A few days passed and I was settling in nicely. I put my female touch on the house. I would clean daily, cook and just bring some character into the house. I remember one day, Tony took me with him to the local supermarket and it felt so weird being around so many people. I felt like I stuck out like a sore thumb. Every noise, every cough, and anyone who got too close startled me. I felt like an alien, but because I was holding Tony's hand, I felt proud and it gave me courage. I started to also notice that during the night, I would see apparitions of Sally. It had happened twice already. It was like some portal that opened in the bedroom and Sally would just appear and gesture to me to come towards her. I would get up and walk towards the light, and the closer I got to it, the quicker it would disappear. That happened many times. I never knew what it meant. Maybe she was telling me she was watching over me. Maybe she was telling me something was wrong at home, I wasn't sure. I knew I would be back to check on them soon.

Things were going great between Tony and I. I was falling more in love with him each day. I had bought a pregnancy test the day we went out and found out that I was pregnant. While we were out shopping, I bravely scampered off to the health and lifestyle aisle by myself. Tony told me it would be okay so I ventured there alone. I was so nervous when I was in the aisle, even though Tony was still there in the supermarket with me. I even dropped the pregnancy test a couple of times whilst trying to pick it up. When I turned around and headed back to where he was last, he wasn't there. I started to panic – the shop seemed to be getting smaller, my heart was racing, and I couldn't breathe properly. I felt so alone again. I was running around the supermarket trying to find him – I was in a terrible panicked state. An older lady asked me if I was okay and I said no, that I couldn't find my partner and just then Tony appeared, calm as ever and he called to me. I was so relieved I jumped on him and hugged him so tight. Things calmed down. Tony had asked me why I was buying the test when I dropped it in the trolley. I grabbed his hand tighter, tilted my head towards him and smiled – I told him about it and he was so excited. I knew he was the man of my dreams. I got home and took the test and while waiting for the result I couldn't sit still I was rocking back and forth, anxiously awaiting the result. Positive. He was so happy when I told him the result. I could see the joy in his eyes. We planned and planned what life was going to be like thereafter.

About two weeks had gone by and I started to notice something very troubling. I kept thinking I could see my mother. Sometimes at night in the bedroom, sometimes in the kitchen, I would see shadows, and in the bathroom, when I was alone, I would hear her voice. It's like she was haunting me. I was so scared. I told Tony about it and he would just cuddle me tight and tell me that everything was okay, which helped a lot. Suddenly, I started to feel a bit depressed. I kept thinking of all the things that my mother had done to me growing up and what she had done to Sally. I would have sleepless nights and I put it down to being pregnant because I couldn't tell Tony all about that; not yet anyway. It was a dark cloud that loomed over me. It would take a long time for it to go away. I think I began having prenatal depression. I was worried about the baby that was to come, if we could cope, if I was capable of being a good mother and just generally worrying about the changes that would come as a result of having this baby. I would have some mood swings and outbursts, but the whole time, Tony was supportive and very loving. He was so amazing. He kept me grounded and he was my rock. I didn't mind whether the baby was a boy or a girl. All I wanted was a healthy baby who was full of energy and was normal. I had another episode of thinking I could see my mom's shadow – it was large and menacing. I started to believe that something was wrong with Tony's house. Maybe there was an evil spirit that was out to get me. I told him about it and he said it was normal and that it was likely due to the stress and emotions I was going through because of leaving my mother's house the way that I did. I just agreed with him and assumed all was okay. I trusted him and I knew he was there to protect me.

Chapter 9

It had been about a month and I had told Tony that I wanted to visit my brother and sister. I was going to show up at the house unannounced because I had no way of communicating with them. I know we did have a house phone, but I figured it wouldn't be worth calling my mother to tell her that I would be coming over, as she would probably tell me not to in her normal rude tone. The best option was to just show up. I hadn't bought them the cell phones yet but Tony had promised me that he would help me get them. I was pregnant, but I always wondered what it was like to work. Just the idea of working to earn your money and being part of a workforce, having colleagues, always interested me. My mother never really worked. She just got state benefits for us. This was because, years ago, she had injured her back I believe. I decided that I was going to go to the house at around 2 pm. Tony was off that day and he was happy to take me to my mother's house to see my siblings. I missed them so much. Besides being in the basement for months, that was the longest time that I had gone without seeing them. I wasn't used to it. However, I was so distracted by my new life that I sort of just got on with things. It got to about 1:30 pm and I started getting myself ready to go and visit them. I also planned on telling my family about the pregnancy. A new addition to the family is always something positive, I thought. The moment we left the house, all of a sudden, I felt nerves fill my body, I broke out in a sweat and my palms got wet. I felt like I was trying to walk to the car but something was pulling me back. It was strange because I always wanted to get out of that house, but I was going back and that made me nervous. But I was with Tony so I knew I was going to be okay. I told him that I preferred it for the time being if he just waited in the car for me. I can only imagine what my mother would have said to him if she saw him. It was a quick drive and we got there nye on 2 pm. From the car, I could see movement in the kitchen so I knew someone was there. I took a minute in the car to gather myself before getting out and approaching the door. I walked up to the door and knocked. About 30 seconds passed and then I heard footsteps approaching – my mother came to the door and asked who it was. When I told her it was me, the first thing she said was, "What are you doing here?" I told her I just wanted to see Timmy and Lizzy. She wouldn't even let me in so I knocked again. "Get lost," she said. "Please, let me see them," I said. I was pleading with her – you could hear the desperation in my voice. She finally relented and opened the door and just walked off. I walked inside and the place still looked the same, although there was a strange smell in the house. It wasn't a bad smell, it smelled like incense which was unusual. I shut the door behind me, slightly heavy handed as I was nervous and walked into the living room. My mom was sitting there just staring me dead in the face as if she wanted me to leave. I saw Timmy and Lizzy who were both as excited to see me as was I to see them. I gave them both the biggest hug and kissed their foreheads. I played with Lizzy's hair as she seemed to have changed it. That's when I noticed that she had a black eye. I didn't want to ask her what had happened so I just ignored it. I knew what had happened. It was my mother's fault. I spoke to them for a few minutes but I could tell by my mother's energy that I wasn't welcome. I asked her if I could use the bathroom and she told me, in an insolent tone, to go ahead. I used the bathroom and just reminisced about growing up in that house. So many bad memories. I quickly snuck into my old room and saw a whole heap of boy's things so I immediately knew Timmy now had that room. I was happy for him. I quickly came back downstairs and then I broke the news to all of them. Mother was stoic and didn't even react. Lizzy and Timmy both recognised that they were going to be uncle and aunt and they were so excited. Lizzy asked me what I was going to call my child and I just said, "I don't know yet." I had a big smile on my face as I held them both tightly. I didn't want to let go. I wanted to take them with me but I knew that wouldn't happen yet. I grew more concerned about Lizzy's eye. It looked terrible and she could hardly keep it open. I just told them both to stay safe and to be careful and that I would see them again very soon. I was hoping that the next time I saw them, I could give them the cell phones and explain to them that they would need to use them discreetly and only to talk to each other and myself. I let them go and told them that I had to go. Lizzy asked me about Tony. I looked at my mother before I answered but she wasn't paying attention. I told Lizzy that he was fine and that they would meet him properly someday soon. She just smiled, gave a slight head-nod and said, "Okay." It was time for me to leave and I didn't know what to say to my mother. She didn't really acknowledge me in the way that I expected her to. But it was what it was. I walked towards the front door; Lizzy begged me to stay for longer. I explained that I had to go but that I would see her very soon. She just looked down at the floor and it broke my heart. I needed to help them get out of that house. I said goodbye to my mother and she just ignored me. Evil cow. I left out the front door and had to take a deep breath and gather myself before I broke down in tears. I walked to the car and just sat inside it. Tony asked me if I was okay and my eyes started welling up. I just told him to take me home, so, he did. We got home and I gave him a big hug before we got out of the car. We embraced for about two minutes and I just started bawling my eyes out. It wasn't hugging him that tipped me over the edge, it was just that I was so safe now. We got inside the house and went straight to the kitchen to start preparing some lunch. Tony wanted to take me out to dinner later on but I told him I was more comfortable staying in. I didn't like being out; I felt exposed as I wasn't used to it yet. I guess he wanted to show me off and I wanted the complete opposite. We ate and just had a siesta on the sofa. For the remainder of the night, we just watched some films and enjoyed each other's company. It was a great night and I was glad that I had seen Timmy and Lizzy. One day, I thought, I could get them to even visit us at Tony's house.

The next day I woke up and had a slight headache. I kept rubbing my temples in the hope that it would help. I remember because it lasted the whole day. I felt the need to tell Tony about all the abuse that I and my siblings had been subjected to. I was sure that he would understand and be there for me. He had always shown a very compassionate side when dealing with me. I was blessed when I met him. We were sitting in the living room and I just suddenly broke down in tears. I couldn't take it anymore. I had to tell Tony about my childhood. I was thinking that I wouldn't tell him every single detail, but I would just give him an idea of what we had gone through. I trusted him and I knew he wouldn't judge me. I was mainly doing it because I had kept it in all these years and had no one to talk to, but also because I wanted to get

Timmy and Lizzy out of there as soon as possible. We sat there and I told him I had something to tell him. We spoke and spoke. I told him everything. I couldn't hold back. He was instantly protective of me and angered by my mother's egregious nature. He consoled me and explained to me that I didn't need to worry about her anymore and that soon we would bring Timmy and Lizzy to his house to live with us. He also advised that I contact the police but I wasn't comfortable doing that. My mom had put the fear of God in me from a young age about reporting her. I thought it would be easier to just sneak them out of the house one night. He disagreed. He kept urging me to contact the police but promised he wouldn't contact them behind my back or without my consent. I decided I was going to leave it and not call them at that time. It was so nice to have someone understand what I had been through, someone who genuinely cared for me and loved me. I was so lucky. For the next few days, Tony would allude to the fact that he was disgusted at my mother's behaviour. He would go into these angry rants about how deplorable she was and how much he loathed her. It felt nice to have him defend me and be on my side, I must admit.

I remember one day, I felt particularly down; my mood was saturnine. I just felt down and I had no idea why. Nothing could put a smile on my face. Tony was so patient with me. He tried everything to make me laugh. He even did an impression of Eddie Murphy, whom I loved, but it didn't make me flinch. I wasn't sure what it was all about but I knew it most probably had something to do with my mother. She had damaged me in a very profound way. I started to fear that I would never be normal because of what I had been through. I kept having flashbacks of all the abuse and neglect and I remembered the day that I tried to run away. I was just a young lady and really still just a child and yearned for a mother's love. But it would never come. It was one thing to have my mother not love me but another to have her hate me too. I started feeling a bit depressed. I wasn't eating much. Tony had to prompt me to eat because I was pregnant. I wasn't talking an awful lot and Tony and I hadn't been intimate for some time. I was worrying that I was going to push him away. He promised me all these things and all I had to do was love him to get them and I felt like I was failing even at that.

One night, I was alone downstairs as Tony had gone to bed early. He had a garden in town he had to work on early the next morning. A nice elderly lady and her husband's place, he told me. I was watching tv and I just suddenly felt this urge to kill myself. It came out of nowhere. It wasn't insidious, it was sudden. I know I was feeling down over the days prior to that but this feeling was so overwhelming. Even as a young child, I didn't have those macabre thoughts. I did once imagine what killing myself would be like, but I had no idea how to. I was trying to shake off this feeling but it grew and grew and got stronger and stronger. Eventually, I decided I was going to do it. I went to the cabinet in the bathroom where Tony kept the medication. I found some medicine that helped to relieve pain and headaches. I stood there and stared into the bathroom mirror – I felt numb and my thoughts were few and far between. I grabbed the medication and just gobbled the whole pack. At first, I didn't feel anything but then I suddenly felt sick, my head started throbbing and my stomach felt strange; my heart started racing and that was all I remembered. I don't remember anything else, just that the next day, I woke up on the bathroom floor where Tony found me. He immediately picked me up, carried me to the car and rushed me to the hospital. We arrived there and I was in a real state of confusion – Tony carried me into the hospital and asked them to summon the doctor. I was asked so many questions by the doctor about if I was being abused, if I was depressed, etc., and I denied everything. He was a nice elderly man who seemed very empathetic. I just explained that I had felt depressed lately and wanted to take my own life. He concluded that it may have been prenatal depression alongside trauma, even though he had no idea about my mother. I didn't dare tell him. 'How did he know so much?' I thought. He did express his concerns though, about the fact that I felt that way and was pregnant. He just advised me to eat particular foods, try to meditate and he gave me a list of websites I could check out that would help me. I was later discharged and Tony took me home. Because of me, he missed his job that day but he called them to rearrange it for a few days later.

I started feeling better. The doctor had prescribed me some anti-depressants which took immediate effect, probably because of the dosage. What struck me as weird was that I had a medical record. People knew I existed. But then that was obvious because I was born in a hospital too. As a child, I wasn't aware of all of this. I thought no one knew I existed and no one would care if I died. As I said, I was beginning to feel better; maybe it was a placebo. Tony cancelled the rest of his work for that week to tend to me and I was so grateful; he was my rock. He is my rock. He would cook, clean and rub my back at night. He doted on me. I was a lucky girl. He really knows how to treat a woman.

A few more days passed and I asked Tony if he wouldn't mind getting me three cheap cell phones. He had one and I needed one to communicate with him, even though we had a house phone, but just in case of emergencies and stuff. I explained that I wanted to give one to each of my siblings so I could keep tabs on them and know what was going on at my mother's house, especially because I wasn't there anymore. I didn't have my own money and I dreaded the idea of going to get one myself. He told me he was more than happy to get them and said he would get them after work that day. I was so grateful. I thanked him and kissed him and then he headed off to work. I did feel a lot better and I was excited about the new phone I was going to get. This way, I could talk to Timmy and Lizzy regularly to make sure they were okay. I assumed using a cell phone would be easy and because they were young, I was sure they would figure it out. I knew they would help each other to understand how to use it. Timmy was always technologically savvy anyway, so I knew he wouldn't have a problem figuring it out. All I had to do was go and visit them again and secretly give them the handheld devices. I planned to go and see them again the next day because Tony didn't have work. When he got home, he gave me the phone and I was on it for hours after he set it up for me. I was so excited that I could use a wireless device to text and call and even email. I didn't have an email address though. He helped me set one up. I had the biggest smile on my face as he was doing the start-up process. It was a small Nokia he got for me and the same but a different model that he got for Timmy and Lizzy. I was so grateful. He is wonderful. I could now talk to them and they would no longer have to be held back by the trope of freedom.

The next day came and again I got myself ready. I was in my first trimester. My stomach was beginning to bulge a bit so I would wear baggy clothing to hide it. Tony and I got into the car and headed to my mother's house at around 4 pm. This time, I wouldn't stay long. We got there and I invariably felt a heap of nerves suddenly hit me. I was worried that my mother wasn't in because the house was extremely quiet. I knocked and I knocked – no one answered. I let myself through the back gate and there I saw Timmy and Lizzy sitting watching tv. My mother wasn't in sight. Perfect! I quietly knocked on the sliding door and Lizzy and Timmy both jumped up in nervous excitement. I gestured by putting my index finger to my lips for them to be quiet. They were. I gestured to Lizzy to open the door and she did. I asked where Mom was and they said she was upstairs taking a nap. Lucky for us. I said I had to be quick and I gave them both hugs. I took the two phones out of the bag and gave one to each of them. I explained to them that the phones were for them and that when Mom was out they should look at the phones. Tony had already pre-set them to silent mode and had already set them both up and written down the numbers. He also wrote down my number and saved it in their phonebooks. I whispered to them to hide them every day and only check them when Mother wasn't around. They acknowledged what I said. I hugged them again and told them I would see them soon. I turned around and headed back to the car without getting caught. I got in and gave Tony a big smile. He smiled back but then he looked upstairs at my mother's window and his face changed. He got angry, clinched his jaw and I saw a vein protrude from his temple. He gripped the steering wheel and almost did a round motion with it. I told him to stay calm and to drive us home. We got home and I already knew Timmy and Lizzy would be engrossed in their phones at night time. They would have fun with them, I was sure of this. I got a text from Lizzy at about 8 pm saying, "Hey, Mary, thank you. I love you," I immediately replied and told her that I loved her too and that she should put her phone away and find a good hiding place for it. She acknowledged this request. I was a bit sad that Timmy hadn't texted me yet, but it was okay because I knew he eventually would. Later, I did text them both goodnight and they both did reply so I was happy.

About two days had passed and I got a text from Lizzy telling me that my mother had slapped Timmy a few times. It was because he hadn't cleaned the toilet after using it. She said it was so bad and we went back and forth via text. I asked her where she was and she said she was in her room and that my mother was downstairs. I told her to be careful so as to not get caught. She told me that my mother was becoming more and more grumpy. As if that was even possible. She was basically bullying the pair of them and she even blamed them for Sally's death. This infuriated me. I couldn't believe that she would stoop so low as to blame them for her own wrongdoing. Coward. It made me sad to read this message. I told Lizzy not to worry and that I would see them again soon. I asked her how home-schooling was going and she said it was going well. She had been doing a lot of work and was enjoying it at the same time. I was happy to hear this. I asked how Timmy was and she said he was just 'Timmy'. Rebellious and defiant, I thought. But other than what had happened, she said he seemed okay. I waited until late at night and then I texted him. I asked if he was okay and how everything was going. He didn't reply until the next morning at around 7 am. He asked me how I was and I asked him the same thing. He told me he was fine and that my mother had just slapped him a few times for not cleaning the toilet after using it, but he was okay so I was okay.

Tony was regularly checking on me after the incident I had with the attempted suicide. He kept a close eye on me and kept texting me while he was at work to make sure I was okay. Luckily, I didn't have another suicidal episode. I felt much better as well. I was looking forward to being a mother and finally extricating my siblings. I was going to make dinner that evening, a roast chicken dinner, and I was excited about feeding my man. He worked so hard to support both of us and I wanted to show him how much I loved him. I cut up some vegetables and cleaned the chicken. I sliced up the potatoes too. It took me a good two hours to prep everything but he loved it; he said it was delightful. We just snuggled and he would rub my stomach every so often. I could tell he was so excited to have this baby and that he would be a great father. Tony spent the rest of the evening telling me about his family. They didn't live far; they lived in Memphis. He had moved out when he was 18 to start his own life. I was very nervous about meeting them because I wasn't very gregarious. I was anti-social because of my upbringing. He didn't put any pressure on me but I knew when the baby was born, I would eventually have to cross that bridge. He also told me about his older brother Steven and how it was just the two of them. I already knew about him but he divulged more information about him, their upbringing, etc. I immediately felt closer to him for opening up to me. He told me a bit about his parents and how life had been as a child. He'd had a good life in comparison to mine. When he realised that he was saying too much, he apologised, but I told him to carry on and that I didn't mind. It was nice to hear about his family and for me to just vicariously live through his experiences. We went to bed early and that night was so strange. During the night, I woke up, rubbed my eyes and yawned. I rolled over and there I saw an apparition of my mother appear in front of me, trying to strangle me in my sleep. I could feel the energy of this entity and it wanted me dead. I couldn't breathe and I was trying to scream but I couldn't get anything out. It was like I was in slow motion and couldn't move properly. It lasted for about 2 minutes but then the entity left me alone. I woke up and immediately woke Tony up and told him that I'd had a bad dream. He hugged me tight and eventually, I fell back asleep. It's like my mother's spirit was haunting me, summoning me back to the house; almost threatening me – how dare I leave? It was so scary and it wasn't the first time this had happened.

The next day I was cleaning the house. I started with the bathroom and then moved to the kitchen, then the living room and finally the bedrooms. I washed sheets, hoovered and polished everything whilst Tony was at work. I was cleaning out the closets and I stumbled upon a box. I wasn't sure of the contents of the box but it felt heavy. I took it out and I opened it, and to my surprise, I saw it was a gun. I dropped it in shock but then gathered myself. I picked up the gun and examined it. It looked like a revolver and the bullets were in there with it. I was shocked. I didn't understand why Tony needed a gun. I put it back where I had found it and I just sat on the bed and spaced out. All these thoughts came into my head. Was he a serial killer? Was he dangerous? I went to my bed and just laid there, quiet and still. I later went downstairs and sat on the sofa and again I was still. I couldn't move. I wasn't sure of how to feel and what to think about this gun. When he got back home, I sat there silently and awkwardly. He kept asking me what was wrong and I eventually broke the silence. I asked him about the gun, his eyes widened and he sighed and looked away for a second, he looked back at me and he explained that it was for protection and that it was normal to have one. At first, I was dubious, but Tony hadn't given me a reason not to trust him so I just believed him. We hugged it out and had a lovely feast.

Later on, I received a text from Lizzy and I asked her how she was. She told me that Mom hadn't found the phones yet but that she had hit her again the day before. I didn't even ask what had happened – I just knew that I had had enough. I couldn't take it anymore. I had tried and failed to kill her, but I was thinking I needed to get them out immediately. Then it hit me. I had it. 'The Gun.'

Chapter 10

Sweat was dripping off my face. I couldn't sit still – I kept shifting in my seat. I knew what I was going to do. I knew it had to be done. I wasn't sure what day I would go there. Ideally, I wanted to do it when Timmy and Lizzy were in their rooms or asleep. I didn't plan on telling Tony about it either because I knew that he would disapprove. Enough was enough. At no point did I even imagine that I would be imprisoned either, because when people found out what my mother had done to us for all of our lives, any jury would exculpate me. Or so I thought. I had set the day; it was going to be on a Sunday, mainly because I knew Timmy and Lizzy went to bed early on Sundays. It was Thursday so I still had three days to change my mind. But I didn't. I couldn't. I was compelled to carry out my plan no matter what it took and nothing was going to stop me. In a way, I had to purge her; it was the only way. For the rest of the day on Thursday, I just thought about what may happen to me if I did go ahead with my plan... if I would be without my baby or imprisoned. I just didn't believe it would happen. I already had a story in my head of what I was going to tell the authorities. I was going to tell them that I went over to the house and I was armed because I never felt safe around her. I would then tell them about all the abuse and that would justify me carrying a gun, even though it wasn't mine. I would then tell them that she attacked me whilst I was there to see my siblings and I had shot her in self-defence. That was my perfect story.

Friday came and I was still determined to carry out my plan on that Sunday. I had made up my mind about it. I was sitting at the dinner table with Tony and I looked deep into his eyes. I think he could tell something was up with me but I was reticent with my thoughts and feelings. I had to keep my cards close to my chest. If he knew, he would mess up the whole plan and not let me go ahead with it. But I'm sure deep down he probably would have felt that she deserved it because of what she had done to us. Whilst we were eating, we didn't talk much to each other. I was playing with my food and hesitating to eat it. Tony asked me what was wrong because I hadn't eaten much of my dinner. I told him that I was just a bit tired and had some cramps. He kept probing and probing but my answer didn't change. He seemed to understand, that whatever it was that was on my mind, I didn't want to talk about it. So, he just brushed it off as I had hoped he would. We finished dinner and walked over to the sofa hand in hand. My favourite movie 'Speed' was on. We watched it together and just forgot about the world. I loved Keanu Reeves' movies. He is a great thespian. We ended up falling asleep shortly after the movie. I woke up to Tony nudging me and telling me to come to bed. I got up and staggered upstairs just ahead of Tony. He was doing his rounds to make sure that all the doors and windows were locked. He always kept us safe. He never took anything for granted. I loved that about him. He is a protector and knows how to make a woman feel safe.

The next morning, I got up bright and early. It was a Saturday and Tony had a few things to do. He also had work. I remember thinking that I wanted to start driving but it wasn't a priority at that point. I do today and haven't looked back ever since. I like being strong and independent and not having to rely on Tony to take me everywhere. It got to about 9 am and Tony was ready to leave. He came over to my side of the bed and gave me a big warm kiss and hugged me. He said bye to me and I just smiled at him. He looked and smelled so good – he had an edge about him but was also very sophisticated which I loved. I missed him when he went out and I worried sometimes that something bad would happen to him. But at the same time, I knew he was out there trying his hardest to provide for both of us. I got up and headed to the bathroom to brush my teeth. I turned on the taps for the bath and then filled up the bathtub. I just laid in there for about an hour and prepared myself mentally for the next day. I could have stayed in the bath forever but then the water started getting dirty and cold. I got out of the bath and dried myself. I creamed myself and put on some house clothes. Then I went downstairs and turned on the television. There wasn't much on so I ended up watching the news for most of the day. We had a VCR and a collection of some old tapes and movies. I rummaged through the plethora of tapes we had and found one titled 'Home Alone.' I loved Macaulay Culkin as a child. From 'Richie Rich' to 'My Girl' to 'Uncle Buck', he was my favourite childhood actor. I just wanted to sit on the sofa and enjoy a nice relaxing day at home with some snacks and movies. I watched Home Alone 1. I just laughed and laughed and had a good feeling inside of me. It took my mind off what I had to do. It was a good distraction because before I started watching the films, that was all I could concentrate on. I didn't like thinking about it over and over again because that would make it all too premeditated. But who was I kidding? It was. I heard keys jangle and the sound got louder and closer. Tony walked through the door. He had a 5 o'clock shadow on his face. He looked worn out and tired and I felt bad for him. He worked so hard. I told him I hadn't made dinner but I was about to. He told me not to worry and that he would order us some local takeaway. I didn't object. A little while later, the food arrived and we indulged ourselves. I was so full that I couldn't even move. Tony wanted to be romantic so he carried me up the stairs and to bed. He made a joke calling me 'a bit heavy'. I gasped and frowned but then he told me he was joking and that he loved me. We both laughed and carried on upstairs, giggling like two love birds as we did. Part of me didn't want to go to bed because that would mean 'tomorrow' was closer. I wasn't confident about it but I knew I had to do it. I lay in the bed and Tony hugged me. I was staring at the ceiling trying to make my thoughts disappear. I finally fell asleep and woke up in the same position. I opened my eyes and it felt like I hadn't slept. Tony got up shortly after and told me he was heading to the gym that morning. That's when I told him that I wanted to go to my mother's house to see Timmy and Lizzy. I said I wanted to go at 10 pm. He then started asking me why I wanted to go so late and I hadn't thought about what I would say if he did ask. I came up with the excuse, that I wanted to avoid my mother and that I would text them to let them know to stay awake and wait for me to come. He agreed and then headed off to the gym. I was staring at his butt as he walked out – I am a lucky woman. I didn't think he needed to work on his physique, he was already so fit. While he was at the gym, I realised that it was time to go and retrieve the gun. I seized the opportunity and went to get it. I had no idea how to use it but it seemed straightforward. I put all the bullets in the barrel and kept it in a secret place – under my dresser concealed under a heap of clothes that I knew Tony would never touch. I knew

Tony wouldn't suspect anything. He got back from the gym about two hours later whilst I was making breakfast for us. It was a nice healthy breakfast with a lot of fruit and fibre. He went upstairs and used the shower before coming down to eat. I was going to take a handbag with me and pretend I wanted to give Timmy and Lizzy some old things that would remind them of our childhood. That was the story I was going to tell Tony because I knew he would ask at some point. He was inquisitive like that and I didn't mind because it showed that he paid a lot of attention to me.

It quickly got to about 8 pm. My baby was due in about five months, in March, and it was quickly approaching Christmas. I was hoping for a lovely Christmas with Tony as we prepared for the new arrival to the family. We ate dinner and then sat and just talked for a bit at the dinner table. It was almost 10 pm and I pretended that I had texted my siblings so they knew I was coming. I went upstairs and grabbed the bag I had packed and picked up the gun from under the clothes where I had hidden it earlier – I was an amateur. I put it in the bag and could feel the weight of it weighing my bag down. I carried it downstairs with me. I told Tony that I was ready to go and he just told me he would be back in a second; he just needed to use the loo. This delay made me more nervous for some reason and my stomach was doing cartwheels. He came back and we headed to the car. It felt like the longest drive ever. I was conscious of every movement, every smell, every sound, but eventually, we got to my mother's house. For the whole drive, I was just holding onto the bag tightly. The plan was I was going to have to shoot her in the front doorway as I knew she wouldn't let me in at that time. How would that work? I had no idea but I wasn't about to back down now – I had come too far.

I got out of the car and shut the door behind me. My hands were shaking so violently that I had to clench my fist to stop the shaking. I walked timorously toward the door. When I got there, I knocked on the door. I saw the passageway light suddenly come on and heard my mother ask who it was. I told her it was me and she asked me what I was doing there. I clutched the gun and was ready to use it. Finally, she opened the door and I just pretended that I had lost track of time and wanted to check on Timmy and Lizzy. She told me that they were already asleep and that I should stop coming around unannounced like that. I apologised to her. We exchanged a few more words and she started insulting me, calling me a w**re and a b**ch. I didn't understand why but it kind of made it easy for me to get angry with her. Then she started saying that Timmy and Lizzy would never see me again and that she would keep them in that house forever. This enraged me. I was seething. I felt for the gun and just kept my hand firmly on it. I had told Tony to park slightly around the corner – out of view. He was sitting in the car waiting for me. I took out the gun and pointed it directly at her. She recoiled and stumbled backwards as I walked inside with it firmly pointed at her. Each step I took forward made her take one back. She started asking me if I was crazy and telling me that I would never get away with it. She then said that because I had tried to kill her before, she would just ignore this episode if I left. I refused. My hand started to shake even more and I was overcome with emotion, rage and sadness. I kept asking her why she had never shown me love and why she treated Timmy and Lizzy so badly. I told her I knew she was still beating them and abusing them and she seemed shocked but had a guilty look on her face. I even blamed her for Sally's death. At this point, we were fully in the living room. My mother started crying and stuck her hand up as if to gesture that she wasn't a threat to me. Yes, she was. She was the devil and I had to get rid of her. We weren't making enough noise for Timmy and Lizzy to hear us, but all I wanted was for them not to see this interaction. I cocked the gun and held my hand steadily. I aimed and just when I heard her say, "NO! NO!"... I just fired at her stomach. I cocked again and fired another round, and again and again. Before I knew it, I had emptied the whole clip until the gun clicked and wouldn't fire anymore. Timmy and Lizzy both peeped out their doors to see what was happening. They were in shock. I told them it was okay and that they didn't have to suffer anymore. Tony ran to the house and asked me what I'd done. He had his hands on his head and swivelled around in disbelief. I just kept repeating that I'd had to do it. I had to. My mother was slumped over and just lying there on the floor motionless. It reminded me of when Sally had died. I did feel remorse but I was also satisfied. I knew she was dead; this time I had succeeded.

Tony got his phone and dialled 911. He was so furious with what I had done. For about five minutes, I just stood there staring at my mother with the gun still in my hand. Tony tried to pry it from my grip but I pulled it away from him. I could hear sirens quickly approaching. I knew what my story was so I wasn't worried. Our house was kind of remote. We didn't have neighbours close by which is why no one suspected anything for all of those years. I could see blue and red lights flashing and reflecting in the woods. Two state troopers arrived and immediately got out. Tony and I were at the front door and Tony approached them as they arrived. "Ma'am… drop the gun!" one of the officers ordered me. Tony turned around to face me and urged me to drop the gun. I was kind of in shock, but when I was conscious of what he said to me, I put the gun down. Tony told them what had happened and they came to me and handcuffed me at the front door – kicking the gun away as they did. They read me my Miranda rights. The gun lay on the living room floor and they detained me and told me I had to go down to the precinct with them. I was like a zombie. I kept saying, "She made me do it... she made me do it." So far, everything was going to plan. I knew I would have to be arrested but when I told them everything about my mother and Sally, they would exonerate me. Tony was so distraught. He asked them if he was allowed to come with me. I interjected and told him to take Timmy and Lizzy to his house for the night until this was all cleared up. I told Timmy and Lizzy to go with him and they did; they trusted me. The look on their faces killed me. They looked so frightened. This was way too much violence for them to have witnessed but I hoped one day they would understand why I had done it. I was put in the police car and I noticed Tony holding Timmy and Lizzy, consoling them. It made me feel better because I knew they were safe. Soon after, the ambulance arrived – to take my mother's body away, I presumed. I knew the coroner would soon arrive. The police car drove off while the other one followed. I put my head down and started crying. I had finally done it. I was willing to sacrifice myself for this cause. I then had a thought in the police car about why I hadn't waited to do it until my baby was born. But that would have meant more months of suffering for my siblings. I knew I had to do it then. I knew they would let me give birth to my baby and that Tony would take care of it. So, in a way, my plan did make sense to me.

We got to the police station and I was ushered out of the car by the policeman. He was white, middle-aged, had a big moustache and a very southern accent; a lot stronger than mine. I was immediately put in a cell by myself. They said they would be inquiring into what happened and would let me know the outcome. I was in the cell pacing up and down. I only had my thoughts with me and nothing else. I could hear several officers in the hallway talking claptrap and making jokes with each other. About an hour passed and I ended up falling asleep on the little bed that was in there. it was so hard and uncomfortable, I don't know how I managed to fall asleep. A little while later, a different policeman came to my cell. He explained that I needed to come to a room where they would ask me questions and get a sense of all that had happened. I thought yes, this was my opportunity to explain everything to them and hopefully, they would have compassion for me and let me go. That simple.

I walked into this little 4x4 room with white walls, a pinewood desk; a tape recorder too. I looked up in the corner of the room near the ceiling and there was a CCTV camera. Straight away, I knew that I had to be aware of my movements and facial expressions and everything that I said and did. I was careful to not look suspicious and to not talk to myself, as I tended to do that quite a lot. The same policeman came into the room and pulled up his chair and sat down opposite me. He explained that it was just an interview to get a sense of what had happened and to hear my version of the events. He started by asking me my name which I told him and then he asked me my mother's name. I answered that too. Then he asked me my address and I gave him Tony's address. He asked my age. Just the formalities. He then asked me in my own words to explain what had happened. I told him the story that I had come up with earlier, that I was there to visit my siblings and that my mother was physically very abusive but

I went armed with a gun for my protection. He then asked me why I took a gun with me and whose it was. I told him it was my partner's gun and that my partner, Tony, had no idea that I had taken it with me. I wanted to make sure they were aware that Tony was completely innocent and not complicit. He then said, "You say your mother is abusive. Can you elaborate on that?" I just told him everything. I told him about the regular beatings we got, about the time she locked me in the basement for five months, about the time she threw stones at us, about the time that she threw Timmy in the basement and everything else. I was compelling and very vivid about everything. By the time I had finished telling him about all the heinous things that my mom did to us, he seemed in shock and he seemed to empathise with me. I hadn't even told him about Sally's murder yet. He then asked, "You said there are four of you. But I only counted three. Where's your other sibling?" I broke down in tears and told him that my mother had killed Sally. That she had strangled her right before our eyes and had made me drive with her over a hundred miles away to dispose of her body and asked me to help her conceal her crime. He reclined in his seat and took a moment to gather his thoughts and feelings. He breathed a deep breath and just shook his head. He then carried on and asked why I had shot her. I explained that when I got to the house, she started to verbally attack me. I had gone there to see my siblings. I had lost track of time but thought it would be okay to go there and see them. After the verbal onslaught, she pushed me and I didn't retort. She pushed me again and dragged me into the house. She had punched me once and then she got up and threatened to kill me. I knew she was capable of doing that based on my past and living with her and the fact that I had seen her kill Sally with my own eyes. So, I believed her. I was scared for my life and I pulled out the gun and asked her to step back. She didn't retreat and she rushed me and I shot her. I didn't count how many times I shot. I just kept shooting and cocking the gun and shooting again, until she was completely still and until I felt there was no more of a threat. I told him that Tony had come to the house because he heard the gunshots and immediately called the police and now here I am. "Okay," he said. Then he told me I would have to make an initial appearance before the judge to be officially informed of the charges I was being held for and for the judge to set a bond. This was to happen the next morning. I agreed and was taken back to my cell. I kept thinking about my unborn baby. I never knew this process would be so protracted but I was still fighting my corner.

The next morning, an officer came to get me and took me to see the judge. He was an elderly white man, who seemed firm but friendly and very calm. He had a soft voice and wore glasses. I felt so intimidated. I hadn't planned for all of this. He told me that I needed to pay a bond. He said, "A bond is an amount of money paid by you (cash bond) or with the help of a bondsman. He or she takes a percentage of cash on the bond issued by the Court (about 10 per cent) and then ensures the remaining amount. A bond is paid to ensure that you will come to Court. If you do not show up for court after "bonding out of jail", then I will issue a bench warrant for your arrest and a judgment will be made that if you aren't arrested, the bond is forfeited. If a bond is set unreasonably too high for you to be released, then your lawyer (who will be appointed by the state if you can't afford one) can request a bond reduction hearing before the judge. There are some instances when you aren't entitled to a bond due to being a flight risk or risk to the safety of the victim. But I don't see this being the case here." It all went over my head. I was just a 17-year-old girl. I had no idea about bonds, etc. I do now that I'm a lawyer. I just nodded and said I understood. He then explained what a preliminary hearing was. He said, "A preliminary hearing is conducted to show whether there is probable cause to hold you in jail until the Grand Jury meets. You will have a preliminary hearing if you cannot successfully be released from jail on bond. If you are released from jail on bond, then there is no right to a preliminary hearing." It was a lot of information to take in, but I knew I had to. Then I thought there was no way I could afford the bond. The only option I had was to get a bail bondsman or for Tony to help me. I was then remanded in custody and then transported to jail. It was a filthy cell I was put into; it was so dirty. It felt surreal being there. But it was real too. Because I was pregnant, I wondered what would happen and also how long this whole process would take and if I would be acquitted before I went into labour. I got my phone call and immediately called Tony who was at home with my siblings, taking care of everyone. It was then that I started to cry, I placed my head against the phone box and sniffed and wiped my nose, I then explained the whole bond process and he said to me that he would ask his parents if they could help me. I asked him why they would help when they hadn't even met me yet; they had only heard about me. I had little faith that it would work. I got off the phone and headed back to my cell and just laid down and prayed. Tony also informed me that his family lawyer could defend me. His name was Michael Watson. He eventually came to meet me and was very friendly and professional. He informed me that the bail was set at $100,000 because I was looking at voluntary manslaughter. So, if I got a bail bondsman, I would have to pay $10,000 upfront which was also non-refundable.

He was eloquent and sharp, and I had faith that he would get me out of this mess that I was in. The next day, I spoke to Tony and told him the news. He said he would speak to his parents and would get back to me. They agreed. I was shocked, firstly by the fact that they had that kind of money and secondly that they were willing to help me, a stranger to them. Bless them, I thought. I asked Michael about my pregnancy and the procedure involving that and he said, "Once the prison confirms the pregnancy, you have **regular appointments with an OB at a hospital outside of the prison. When you are transported, you will wear handcuffs and shackles**. When you go into labour, you are transported to a hospital so they can deliver – if there is enough time." I understood. They had me wearing these hideous beige overalls whilst I was there. I was a prisoner again just like in my mother's house. There was no need for a preliminary hearing as the bond was paid by Tony's parents, with him also contributing to it. They were such good people and I looked forward to being part of their family.

I was released on bond and Tony came to pick me up. I was so relieved to see him. He gave me a big hug and we went home. I saw Timmy and Lizzy; they were still shaken up but happy to see me. My case was moved from the local town to a Circuit Court. It was Lee County Circuit Court as I was indicted by the grand jury. I was informed that the grand jury had met up and I was informed that the state of Mississippi had sufficient evidence to fairly require me to answer to and defend against a felony charge. It wasn't a misdemeanour as that would only require me to be in jail for up to a year. This was a lot more serious. I was then issued with a felony capias and indictment. The sheriff served me with a copy of the capias and indictment with a list of charges and a date to appear before the Circuit Court. It was two weeks from that day. I remember vividly. Because the sheriff trusted me and understood my plight, he allowed me to pick up my capias and indictment, rather than be arrested and go through that process again.

It was the day of the arraignment. I had to appear before Lee County Circuit Court and decide whether to plead guilty or not guilty to the charges stated in the indictment from the grand jury. I pleaded not guilty of course. It was all happening so quickly, like a rollercoaster. I had to keep my emotions in check. As I mentioned, my attorney, Michael Watson, was very well-spoken and sharp. He was fairly young but he knew what he was about and I had faith in him. He was Tony's family lawyer and I was lucky enough that his parents had hired him for me. Michael then kept explaining the whole procedure to me. He requested a discovery, which was all the evidence the state of Mississippi had on the felony case. He gave me a copy and we met up a few days later to review it. I was nervous. I couldn't stop fidgeting but he kept me calm. There was a plea deal I could have taken which would have come with a mandatory 7-year sentence, but in the end, I refused to accept that because I wanted to be with my family. Because I refused the plea deal, we then had to submit a reciprocal discovery to the DA's (District Attorney) office. What it basically meant was both sides must submit before trial any evidence they plan to introduce at trial in the discovery process, or risk that evidence not being admitted at trial. This all happened because I had decided to go to trial rather than accept the plea deal. I was going to plead not guilty and nothing was going to change my mind. My mother was wicked and I killed her in self-defence in the end.

About a month after I got arrested, the trial started. The trial was lengthy and difficult. The jurors were a mixed bag. Some looked like working professionals, some looked like single mothers. Just a variety of people. I preferred women as opposed to men because they would sympathise with me more when they learned what my mother had done to me.

The trial went on for two days. Timmy and Lizzy both had to testify. They were both so nervous but I knew it strengthened my case against my mother. They were compelling and incited emotion in the jury, I could tell, especially when Lizzy told the story of how my mother beat her so badly for making a mess in the kitchen. It moved me because it made me remember all of those horrific days. Both of them told the prosecutor and Michael everything they could about what had happened to them. Michael explained that the stand-your-ground law may apply and then he also mentioned something about 'The Castle Doctrine' and 'Cessation of Threat' which both helped my case.

It was my turn to testify. I was also cross-examined about premeditating the act because I brought the gun along with me, but I think I convinced the jury that I was always in fear for my life around my mother, and, after she killed Sally, I was even more so. I told them everything – about all the different times I was verbally and physically beaten and abused. I told them about Sally and all my siblings and I could see some of the jury members tearing up. They were just so sad because of what I had gone through. I told them about when I was locked in the basement for five months and everyone gasped. I told them about how we never integrated into society and how we were raised like prisoners; how we were hardly allowed to watch tv and got beaten for getting work wrong when we were home-schooled. I told them about the time my mother burnt me with cigarette butts, about the time when she put me in a freezing cold bath, and about the time she shoved a broomstick up my private part. They were in shock; they were on my side. I told them about the times my mum would beat Timmy and refuse to give us food. They were gripped. Some of them had their eyes closed, visualising what I had gone through and how they would feel if it was them or their kids. I told them about when I tried to run away; I even told them about the time I tried to kill my mother because I felt I had no other option. I told them everything. Everything! The judge seemed stern but sympathetic. He made his final statement and it seemed that he understood my plight and why I had killed my mother. It was clear that there were extenuating circumstances around this case.

It was the day of the verdict and I was so nervous. I really wasn't sure what It would be. I was afraid and worried. I hoped that I had said enough to convince them to acquit me of any crime. I kept my head down most of the time and couldn't even bear to look anyone in the face.

NOT GUILTY!! It was unanimous. I burst into tears and couldn't believe it was finally over. I jumped up and hugged Michael then I went to Tony and hugged him. I had met his parents before the trial started; they were as lovely as I thought they would be and I hugged them too. I reached out to Timmy and Lizzy and we all embraced each other. It was done. I was relieved I could finally close that chapter of my life and move on. The judge told me I was free to go and those words were like music to my soul. I was free. I was heavily pregnant at the time and it wasn't long until I was to give birth. Not long after, I settled back into life at home with Timmy, Lizzy and Tony. It took me a while but I was getting better. Timmy and Lizzy had the two rooms and Tony and I had the master bedroom. Soon after, we got a golden retriever puppy.

We called him Max. He was so energetic and beautiful. We all loved him and he was a joy to be around. I regularly saw Tony's parents and eventually met his brother too. We went on several outings, had a lot of picnics and just did a lot of outdoor activities. I felt a lot better about myself and I was on the road to recovery. I would still occasionally have flashbacks but I was told that was normal. I found out the baby was going to be a boy. Tony and I decided to name him Bobby. Not long after all of this, Tony and I got married. It was a small ceremony but was beautiful.

We started early with the decorating of our bedroom for Bobby's arrival. Almost every time we went out, we would buy something for him. I was so excited. I did all of this to make sure that he would have a good life, one that I never had growing up. I was with a good man who loved me and who I knew would love our son. We had gone to the ultrasounds and all the baby classes as a lot of this happened after the trial. One evening, I could feel a sharp pain in my stomach while I was sitting on the sofa watching tv. I stood up to try and shake it off but it was incessant. Tony offered to get me some water and I thanked him. I drank it but it didn't help. The pain persisted. I thought it was Braxton Hicks but I was having real contractions. About 30 minutes later, my water broke. Suddenly, there was a big puddle underneath me. The pain was excruciating but I knew Bobby was almost home. Tony helped me get into the car, and in a hurry, he drove me to the hospital. We took Timmy and Lizzy with us. We got to the hospital and went straight in. I was concentrating on my breathing as I was taught this at the antenatal classes that I had attended. I was being looked after by a very nice female doctor who asked me if it was my first child. I told her it was, and somehow, she calmed me down so much that I forgot about the pain I was in. Not long after, I was in labour. I was excited but nervous. I just hoped he would be a healthy boy. I didn't go for a C-Section. I just pushed and pushed as the doctor advised me to. it was so painful. And then, just like that, I heard him crying. They cut the umbilical cord, wrapped him in something and put him in my arms. He was beautiful. He was finally born. Holding him in my arms was the happiest moment of my life. The birth was painful but so beautiful. I have never felt such love like that before. Shortly after, Timmy, Tony and Lizzy all came in with wide smiles on their faces. They all greeted little Bobby and showed him so much affection, it was so nice to see. Heart-warming. We figured that Timmy and Lizzy would eventually move out. They were getting older and we thought we could convert one of their rooms into Bobby's when he got a bit older.

Chapter 11

Many years had passed and I had been blessed with a second child; a daughter, Emily. My children were five years old and two years old. Bobby is, of course, the older of the two. We are now living in Lawrence, Indianapolis in Indiana. We live with our dog Max who is now much older, but he is still as adorable as he was when he was a pup. He is very playful and protective, especially over my kids. I set up my own charity which works with children who suffer from abuse and also adults who suffered from abuse as children, just as I did. It's called 'New Horizons'. Tony helps me with it here and there but I predominantly run it. We set up the charity in Indiana, Indianapolis. So I've moved from a small town to a big city. It was a big change to begin with but I have gotten used to it now. I decided to use my vicissitudes to help less fortunate people out. I am a vehicle for change and rehabilitation for people who weren't or aren't able to help themselves. I decided that I wanted to do this to bring change to the world. No one was able to help me, so I figured I could help people. I also decided that I wanted to become a lawyer, to help bring justice to the world even in a small way. It took several years to complete all of the requirements for my Juris Doctor (J.D.) professional law degree. I attended the Indiana University Robert H. McKinney School of Law in Indianapolis, which held the ABA accreditation. I went into criminal law. I did my 90 hours of semester hours too. I took my Bar exam in July 2003 and passed that too. I had to do the Indiana Essay Examination, the multistate performance test (MPT), and the Multistate Bar Examination (MBE). I had to pass my Multistate Professional Responsibility Exam (MPRE) once I had completed my Indiana Bar Exam. I had to wait for my Bar exam results to arrive in the post and I was so nervous because I didn't know when they would arrive. I would check the post regularly and would walk nervously toward the post box, then, when I got there, I would take a deep breath and check the mailbox. It took about two months to arrive. I remember the day that they finally came, my hands were shaking and I could hardly breathe. I was hyperventilating, but when I finally opened it and saw that I had passed, I was so ecstatic. Tony and I had a drink that night to celebrate. I then had to attend my swearing-in ceremony which went something like this:

"I do solemnly swear or affirm that: I will support the Constitution of the United States and the Constitution of the State of Indiana; I will maintain the respect due to courts of justice and judicial officers; I will not counsel or maintain any action, proceeding, or defence which shall appear to me to be unjust, but this obligation shall not prevent me from defending a person charged with crime in any case; I will employ for the purpose of maintaining the causes confided to me, such means only as are consistent with truth, and never seek to mislead the court or jury by any artifice or false statement of fact or law; I will maintain the confidence and preserve inviolate the secrets of my client at every peril to myself; I will abstain from offensive personality and advance no fact prejudicial to the honour or reputation of a party or witness, unless required by the justice of the cause with which I am charged; I will not encourage either the commencement or the continuance of any action or proceeding from any motive of passion or interest; I will never reject, from any consideration personal to myself, the cause of the defenceless, the oppressed or those who cannot afford adequate legal assistance; so help me God."

I completed a mandatory six hours of applied professionalism coursework in my first three years of membership. I then joined the Indiana State Bar Association's Young Lawyers Section which has helped me to become a successful lawyer and I eventually plan on setting up my own practice. I started working for Jill Goldenberg – Cohen Garelick & Glazier – who covered many different courts under the Indiana Court System. I became certified by an independent certification organization (ICO) approved by CLE. After years of working there, I even received an AV rating** under the Martindale-Hubbell peer review rating process, the highest rating available for legal excellence and ethical practice. So, without tooting my own horn, I became quite successful as a lawyer. My life was looking a lot more structured and meaningful. Tony and I were happier than ever, and he would still do the most romantic things for me. He would bring me flowers and just surprise me from time to time to keep me on my toes. It was titillating. Life was really good. Every night, I would make sure that dinner was cooked for my whole family. I loved the fact that we could all sit together every day and eat together. It meant a lot to me. When I was young, my family was disjointed and rather separated. I loved the sense of closeness. It filled me with a lot of joy. I showered my kids with doting love and affection. We would celebrate birthdays every year and we would regularly go to the park or amusement parks for the kids. Tony is a very loving father. I couldn't have asked God to have given me a better man. I got into trans meditation as well as I heard it was good for the mind and body, centring your thoughts and keeping you grounded. I would usually do it every morning without fail.

Times had really changed since when I was young. Technology was far more advanced and everything was just a click away. I bought myself the latest phones and laptops and would use them every day, from planning work events to putting reminders in for birthdays, etc. Not that I would forget such important dates anyway. I remember when Tony's 31st birthday was coming up. I really wanted to make it special for him and thank him for all he had done to save my life, just to thank him for being there for me, for being an outstanding father and for all the love that he gave me every day. I had come such a long way from where I was when I was a teenager. For his 30th birthday, I planned a trip for all of us to Disneyland in Florida. The weather was beautiful and we loved every minute of it. When the kids were asleep, Tony and I had a romantic dinner and ate such lovely food. It was the best day I had ever had with him and the kids. I will never forget it. As I said, we celebrate all birthdays and made it a thing that we always do. There was never the excuse of "I'm too tired" or anything like that – never a dull moment. We made those days priority dates and always enjoyed them.

I didn't quite know what to do for his 31st birthday. I was thinking of taking him on holiday, but it was coming up quickly and I had to plan it properly. Timmy and Lizzy were in school. Timmy was soon to attend university. He didn't go straight into it after high school. Instead, he took some years out to work menial jobs to save up some money before he went off to university. They also live in Indiana but Timmy is in shared accommodation and Lizzy has her own place. Lizzy works as a nurse but intends on becoming a doctor one day.

It's her dream. She wants to become a paediatrician to help young children, which I think is laudable. Timmy is good at fixing things. When they lived with us, he fixed so many things in the house. His gut was telling him to go into engineering or mechanics. But Timmy has changed a lot; he is quite antisocial and very reserved. He is reticent and doesn't talk a lot when I see him. I really worried about him and about how he was coping with the trauma we suffered as children. I also found out that Lizzy had a new boyfriend. They had been dating for some years and seemed good together. I remember when I found out, I was so excited for her – you should have seen me – I was elated, I was jaunty and I couldn't stop talking to her about him. I wanted her to tell me everything and describe him. We really bonded that day. Timmy still didn't have a girlfriend as far as I knew, or if he did, he kept it to himself. He was a bit reclusive and very private. I understand being that way so I never questioned him about why he was so quiet. I let him be himself. The last thing I wanted to do was pressure him into being someone he didn't want to be, just for my sake. That wouldn't have been fair. Over the years, we all got along very well living at Tony's place after the trial and everything that happened. We got to enjoy the town of Raymond and integrate with society. I finally went to school and so did my siblings. I even made some friends who I still speak to today. I'm still very wary of women, however, and I always seem to keep everyone at a certain distance for my own protection. Today, my closest friend is Megan. We went to law school together and we keep in regular contact. Honestly, though, I'm so busy with my work and kids that I don't get to see her very much at all. I tried to reach out to my father using the internet. I didn't manage to find him. Maybe one day... it would be nice to find out why he abandoned us when we were so young. Had he been around, maybe things would have been very different in our home, just having another person to act as a distraction for my mom or to be a guide and prevent her outbursts, etc. In a way, I also hoped that he would somehow find me. I still yearned for that parent/child relationship because it's something I missed out on. I never tell my children about their grandmother. They only need to know about Tony's mom. She is so sweet and loving. She would help anyone and has a big heart. I did tell them about my dad. Although I couldn't remember much about him – I told them his name and that he had to go away when I was a young child around Bobby's age. I was trying to put across the message that I would never leave them. I didn't demonise him but I explained that if you can't love your child, maybe you should give them up to someone who will show them a lot of love. That's what every child needs. All I knew was that I was going to be there for them through everything. I'd teach them how to drive, I would teach them how to ride a bike, and I would talk to them about their first crush. I would just be there for them always and forever.

In my charity 'New Horizons', I grew attached to this little girl who had run away from home. We picked her up one day while driving through the city. She was hunched up against the wall sitting outside a shop with a tear rolling down her little face. We approached her and asked her what she was doing there. At first, she didn't speak. She was broken and alone. We managed to call for some help and she was adopted by a nice family here in Indiana, the 'Parsons'. Her name is Cynthia; she is part of our group now and she comes to our meetings regularly. I'm so fond of her – her courage, her attitude and her character. She reminded me of a small me. The reason she was on the street was because she was being abused sexually by her stepfather and her mother knew about it and did nothing to protect her. She allowed it to happen and would abuse her too. I felt so bad for her. A part of me wanted to even adopt her at some point, but it never worked out that way. I'm just glad that she got adopted and now is working on becoming a better person and helping others by telling her story. She is one of the main reasons why I started the charity years later. It's one thing to go through it yourself, but when you see yourself in someone else, it makes you stir your stumps and kicks you into gear to take action. One man's story is every man's story as they say.

There are other members in the club. There's Margie, an adult now in her forties, who was abused by her mother as a child. She is lovely; she has brown hair, wears glasses and always wears flowery dresses. She is demure and shy but has a big heart. There's Ray who is very tall, about 6'7, he has an army haircut, has the nose of a boxer, a very gaunt face and an interesting sense of style. I always used to laugh at what he wore. He would wear ripped jeans with tank tops or boots with skinny jeans in the brightest colours. It amused me but he didn't mind me cackling about that. As a teenager, he was abused by his stepfather. There are many more members that I could mention. We meet up fortnightly in a community centre that they gave us in the city. The meetings have really helped a lot of the members, including myself. I used my experience to teach them what I know. As I said, Tony also comes from time to time and is more like moral support. He is great and so altruistic – I picked the right man. I always say that to everyone I meet. At the end of the day, we all need help and there's nothing wrong with reaching out to get it in whatever form it comes in. You will be surprised that the person that can help change your life is the person that you least expected to. We got more and more people joining the club and I still run it today. If I'm honest, I do have my day job but this club is the most important and meaningful thing to me as far as what I do. I don't see it as work; I see it as helping people that need help.

One other member we have is Judy who used to self-harm when she was a teenager. She is slim and petite, she always wears designer clothing and sports sunglasses as often as she can. She has a hoarse voice and is a heavy smoker. She used to get beaten and molested by her dad so much that she got pregnant with his child. She had an abortion, but the years of trauma and suffering made her turn to self-harm. Once, she told us a story about how she tried to slit her own wrists. She couldn't take the torture anymore. She just wanted the pain to end. I have so much respect for her. I can imagine how that must have felt, to be so violated and so betrayed by someone who you are supposed to trust the most and who is meant to protect you from people precisely like that. I had a soft spot for Judy. She reminded me of me in a way and I empathised with her. She was finally able to get away from the abuse because she mustered up the courage, one day, to call the authorities and she was removed from the house that she was living in.

In our group, we have a lot of exercises that we do for both the adults and the kids, separately. We have lessons, like ways in which one can manage anxiety and trauma, what one should do if they are getting abused, how to notice signs of abuse, and so on. I find it helpful and I think the group does too. I'm constantly getting feedback from them telling me how much the classes are helping and have changed their lives for the better.

As I was saying, Tony's 31st birthday was fast approaching. I wanted to do something grand for it. I had a lot of ideas in my head about what I could plan and finally decided that a trip for five days to The Bahamas was the best choice. It would be lovely. I would have liked to have gone for longer but work commitments didn't permit that. We would leave Bobby and Emily with Tony's parents and just have time to ourselves. It was done. I went online and started looking at beautiful resorts in The Bahamas. The scenery was so idyllic and peaceful. I knew we would have a great time there. I found a reasonably priced resort and I just went ahead and booked it. I had to be stealthy; I didn't want Tony to even have the slightest clue about what I had planned. The day before the trip he would just come home and I would tell him to pack his bags and we would leave the next day. That was my plan. Over the years, I had learned that Tony is a typical man – he doesn't like surprises. But I didn't care; I wanted to do this for him. He deserved it and then some. I went behind his back and called his mother to arrange this secret trip. She was more than happy to have Bobby and Emily for the five days that we were away. They would stay at their house until we came back.

The day came for the big surprise. Tony had gotten home, tired, at around 7 pm. I greeted him at the door and gave him a big hug and a kiss. He was such a man, so muscular and masculine. He smelled like aftershave and sweat but I loved his scent. My pheromones were going crazy. I grabbed him by the hand and led him to the sofa – his hands were so strong and manly. Bobby and Emily were already upstairs getting ready for bed. I sat him down and just stared him in the eyes. I asked him how his day was at work and he said it was long. I smiled and moved closer to him then kissed him on the cheek. I told him not to worry and that his birthday was the next day and that I had a surprise to tell him. He asked me what it was and I was teasing him with my eyes and my smile. I told him to guess. "You got me a watch? You got me a new gardening toolset?" I shook my head in excitement – I was so pleased with myself that he had no clue. He was waiting in anticipation for me to tell him what I had gotten for him. I asked him where was the one place in the world that he would want to go to. His face lit up and a wide smile appeared. He said, "Anywhere on an island that's hot and relaxing". I stopped the suspense and told him we were going to The Bahamas the next day. His jaw dropped to the floor. He was so excited. Tony rarely showed emotions outside of his own feelings, but to see that smile on his face, I knew I had picked the right gift for him. We hugged for about two minutes and he kept telling me how excited he was and how much he loved and appreciated me. He had a million and one questions about the logistics of it all and how long we would be there, how I had afforded it, etc. I just told him to be quiet and kiss me and so he did. We had a passionate night together and we got ready early the next morning for our trip. It was the best time ever. Blue waters, white sands, fruit cocktails, salads, fresh seafood and Caribbean cuisine. And of course alcohol. It was everything we could have dreamed of. Oh, I forgot to mention to you that Tony occasionally smoked, but usually only when he had a lot of work. He did indulge in a few cigarettes in The Bahamas but I didn't mind. I wanted it to be about him and for him to enjoy himself. My mother was a smoker, so I am surprised to this day that I am not. They say you are more likely to smoke if one or both of your parents smoke. For most of the holiday, we just laid on the beach basking in the sunlight. We would be there from morning till night. It was beautiful. From the minute we got there, I immediately knew we would go there again and maybe this time with the kids, so they could experience it too. While I was there, I started having some stomach cramps so I started wondering if I was pregnant again. I didn't mind. I wanted to have at least four children anyway. I was with the man of my dreams, so why would I mind?

After the holiday, we landed, went through airport security and then headed to our house. We were a bit jetlagged. The plan was that the next day we would pick up Bobby and Emily from Tony's parents' house. We just spent most of the day in the house talking, relaxing and enjoying the little bit of freedom we had to spend with each other. It felt like how it did when we were younger, with no responsibilities and nothing to worry about or think about but each other. It was full of passion. It was like re-igniting the spark that we had. It was important and it is important that in a relationship you never stop making an effort. Where a lot of people go wrong is they get lazy and stop making the effort to show their partner how much they love them. The next day was a Saturday. We woke up nice and early, got ready and went over to Tony's parents' house. We spent the day there just playing board games and watching movies. I gave my kiddies such a big hug – I had missed them dearly. There's no better feeling in the world than being a mother. It's why when I became a mother, I couldn't understand why my mother hated it so much. It isn't easy being a parent, but a lot of it is innate. You learn as you go. No mother is perfect, but what you do is try your best to raise your children the right way and to the best of your ability. We had a lovely time there and we were telling everyone about the trip and how beautiful it was. We told Bobby and Emily that we would take them there one day and they seemed excited at the idea. They seemed to have missed us because they couldn't let go of us when they hugged us.

We had a nice dinner and all ended up going to sleep quite early. Tony's parents had a huge house with several bedrooms, so we stayed in one of the bedrooms and had a lovely night's sleep. The next day, we got up bright and early and we all started getting ready to head back home. We looked forward to getting back home and getting back to our routine. Bobby had school the next morning anyway, so we couldn't stay for longer. We got our stuff ready and said our goodbyes to Tony's parents. We thanked them for looking after the kids and we left. When we got home, Bobby and Emily were so excited. I had brought back some souvenirs. I told them both that I had got them something and they were just so excited to get back home to find out what it was. I bought Bobby a little snow globe with the Bahamian flag in it and I bought Emily a little doll that had their culture. She loved it and wouldn't stop playing with it when we got back home. During the journey in the car, Bobby kept asking what I had got for him. He couldn't wait. I told him to be patient and that he would love it, but he kept moving around in the backseat; he was restless and excited. I found it so sweet. This is something I never had the luxury of being able to look forward to as a child so I understood it. My mother never surprised us with anything when she went out and came back from town. So, it was lovely to see the look on Bobby's face. He loved the snow globe I got for him and Emily couldn't leave her doll alone. She would plait its hair, give it new outfits and she even named it – she named her doll Sally after her late aunt. I always told them good things about their late aunt Sally, but obviously, I never told them about how she met her demise. However, they knew she was lovely and warm. They would have loved her. It's a shame she wasn't around to meet them. Sally was always the smartest amongst us; she had the most potential and she had a lot going for her.

Chapter 12

Life was great. Everything was copacetic. Some more years passed and the kids were growing up so fast. Bobby was about ten years old and Emily was seven. Unfortunately, our dog Max had passed away. We missed him dearly. He was a part of the family. The kids loved him too. Bobby was going to a local school near where we lived. He was in grade five at the time. Bobby attended HL Marshman Middle School. His favourite subjects were Maths and Science. He is a smart boy and loves anything to do with those subjects. Tony and I used to joke around, saying that one day he would work for NASA. He had the capability to do so. Some of the things he would say made me realise how smart he was, even at that young age. It was lovely to see my kids growing up and developing their own identities. Emily had just started going to primary school and loved it. She was so excited to go to school every day and interact with the other kids, something I never had the opportunity to do growing up. So, I was happy for her. One day, when Bobby was eight, I received a call from his school. They told me that he had gotten into a fistfight with one of his classmates. I gasped in horror when I received that phone call. I didn't know what it was about but I later found out that Bobby was getting bullied by this boy who was bigger than him. I hate bullies; my mother was a bully and you know how that turned out. I was called into the school to have a meeting with Bobby, the boy, his parents, and the headteacher. They seemed like nice enough people but the mother was somewhat imperious I found. She kept on defending her son and made it out that in her eyes, he couldn't do anything wrong, which I felt wasn't fair. But I understood that because I also defended Bobby's actions. I stressed the fact that he was being bullied and felt like he had to defend himself, which is why he hit the boy, whose name is George, in the first place. This was the first time that Bobby had ever complained about such an issue or that he had assailed someone in his school. Growing up, he was very calm and laid back. He wouldn't hurt a fly, so I knew the bullying must have been incessant for him to react that way. After that incident, Bobby didn't have to deal with George again. The headteacher forced them to bury the hatchet, shake hands and makeup. So, they were no longer at each other's throats. I was alarmed but satisfied. I left the meeting and later on, I had a word with Bobby about what had happened. Being a parent isn't easy – no one tells you what you are supposed to do in certain situations. You just learn as you go and you do what you think is best. I made sure to not take what had happened for granted. I asked him what actually happened and why he had reacted in the way that he did. He explained that George would constantly badger him and pick on him in class and in the playgrounds at the school. For a long time, Bobby just ignored him. He had asked him several times to stop and even threatened George that he would report him to his teacher. But push came to shove and Bobby finally said enough was enough and struck him. I told Bobby to never let anyone take his freedom away. I told him that bullies are cowards. They are weak people who try and put vulnerable people down to make themselves feel stronger or more important than them. He seemed to understand what it was that I was trying to say. I also told him to promise me that if it ever happened again, he would talk to me first before he reacted. He promised. I told him that I loved him and that I would always be there for him if he needed me. I told him that he was special and that no one had the right to intimidate him. I told him that was just something that a privileged child is most likely to do, but in life, bullies come in all shapes and sizes and they can bully you in different ways.

One day, Bobby had misbehaved at home. He then tried to lie to me about it too. What happened was that he had broken a game console that I got for him because he was enraged about the game cheating him. I heard a loud crash coming from upstairs in his room. He smashed the controller and then smashed that into the console rendering it unusable. He then tried to lie to me, by saying that it happened by accident and that he was jumping up and down and he accidentally stood on the console in the process. I was furious with him. I had never ever been so angry with him before. I remember that day because I snapped. I don't know where the anger came from but I didn't like what it reminded me of... her. It all started with Bobby being in his room and playing his game. Emily was downstairs watching cartoons and I was in the kitchen as I was off that day. Tony was at work. He was so stalwart. I heard a loud scream coming from Bobby's room and a thud soon after. I went upstairs to investigate as I was concerned that he had hurt himself. Upon opening his door, I saw that he was sitting there with his head in his hands. He seemed sad that his console was no longer working. At first, I thought it had something technically wrong with it but then I looked closely at it and saw that there was a huge dent and crack on the top of it. I asked him what had happened, then he explained that he was playing the game and because he got so excited, he was jumping around next to it and ended up stepping on it inadvertently. At first, I believed him. But I know my son – he had a guilty look in his eyes and I told him to tell me the truth and that I wouldn't be angry with him. That was it. I wouldn't have been that angry if he was honest with me. I kept asking and he kept lying. My eyes were probably bloodshot – red and filled with rage, and I eventually started shouting at him. It was rare for me to shout. I had done it a few times to both Emily and Bobby, but like I said, it was rare. It was important to me that my children did respect me and didn't take me for granted, but I never wanted to be a stringent type of parent. I didn't feel that was necessary. I grew angrier and angrier with Bobby the more he denied what he had done. I was so frustrated. I started yelling even louder at him and I got in his face. He was defiant and told me that he didn't do anything wrong and asked me why I was shouting at him. I grabbed his arm and told him that if he didn't tell me what he had done, I would confiscate all of his toys and he would have nothing to play with at all. He started crying and I told him to stop acting like a little girl. He shouted at me and I just snapped. I slapped him in the face twice. He started crying even more and screaming this time.

As soon as I hit him, I immediately felt horrible. I felt my heart sink and there was a clunk of saliva in the back of my throat as I tried to come to grips with what I had done. I knew what I had done was wrong, and at that moment, I reminded myself so much of my mother. I held him and apologised to him. I even started crying my-self when I realised what I had done. I felt so guilty and Emily came upstairs and peeked through the door. She saw me hugging Bobby and both of us crying. She asked what was wrong and I told her that everything was fine and that she should go back downstairs to watch her cartoons. I never got over that incident. Emily left. Bobby had his head down. I lifted his head up and told him that I would never hit him again and that I was so sorry. He seemed crestfallen with me. I could see in his eyes that the trust between us had been somewhat broken. It was up to me as his mother to fix it. And I did. We hugged for a while and I just kept kissing his forehead and reminding him how much I loved him. He seemed to be warming up to me again. In a low innocent voice, he asked if he could get another console. I gave him a cheeky smile – one of contempt but also of penitence. I told him that I would get him a new console but that he needed to control his rage when it came to things like that. I taught him that violence was never the solution to anything because once you get physical, you have already lost. It takes more to not react to things than it does to react to things. We sat there for a minute and I asked him how he was generally and he said he was okay. We headed downstairs hand in hand and I saw the concerned look on Emily's face. She wore a frown and the corners of her lips were arched upwards. She asked me if everything was okay and I explained that Bobby and I just had a little talk and that everything was fine. I hugged her to mollify her. She felt a lot better soon after. We ate some food and just waited for Tony to come back home. When Tony got home, I was a bit concerned that Bobby would tell him what had happened and that he would misunderstand what I was trying to do. So, after dinner, I told Tony the whole story myself. He seemed shocked, but he understood and told me that I need not worry about it and that he loved me. He recognised that I felt bad about it because of what I had gone through with my mother and he empathised with me. I just hated the fact that, at that moment, I was behaving like my mother always did. It's like I had become her and, from that day onwards, I made a vow to myself to never hurt any of my kids again. It never happened again. Anytime they frustrated me or angered me, I would make sure to never scare them into feeling like I had when I was a child. I didn't allow myself to do that to them. It was important to me that they always felt loved. For the rest of the night, I felt a bit sad. I just reminisced about some of the horrible things I was put through. I was lucky to have Tony there. He really did take my mind off everything as he so often did. He cuddled me to sleep and I felt safe and protected again. It's one of the best feelings in the world.

I remember a few days later, Bobby was meant to be going to the party of one of his friends called Todd. It was Todd's 10th birthday; he was slightly younger than Bobby, but they had been good friends since primary school. I just wanted Bobby to have fun and spend time with his friends. I had never really had friends growing up, so it was important to me that my kids had good friends and positive influences around them, outside of Tony and me. In the world we live in today, kids can be very mean. Bullying is very common and people can leave you feeling isolated just like that. But from what I knew about Todd, he was a good boy and he came from a good home. His parents' names are Barry and Amanda. They are also a middle-class family with good values and morals. Bobby was so excited to go to the party – he could hardly contain his excitement. He went to the party and had a great time. He seemed so happy when he came back home and it filled me with joy. I asked him how the party was and he told me it was fun and that they played games and ate a lot of cake and food. He enjoyed himself. When Bobby was born, I was very protective of him. It reminded me of my little brother Timmy. I wanted to do better at being there for him because I know when it came to Timmy, there were times when I wasn't there for him in the way that I could have been.

I would always monitor everything that Bobby did, from the cartoons that he watched, to who his friends were, to what sort of toys he would play with. I was a tiger mom and I still am to an extent. It's the only way I know how to parent. Tony is a lot more laid back and casual about being a parent; it seems more natural to him I think – but it's nice that we have a balance. Good cop, bad cop, sort of. Every day Bobby went to school, I'd always ask him in detail about his day at school, if he'd had any trouble or if anyone was bothering him. My worst fear was that he was being bullied or something of that sort. One day, when he was about six, he came home from school and he had a very sad look on his face. He had his head down and his bottom lip was puckered outwards beyond his upper lip. The whole time he was home he was reclusive and anti-social. I probed and asked him what was wrong and what had happened at school and after about an hour of me insisting on him telling me, he finally told me what had happened. He told me that all the kids were playing and there came a point where they had to pick teams for a game of rounders and he wasn't picked. He felt left out, sad and almost embarrassed. I explained to him that he was special and that he need not worry about that incident. It wasn't personal; it's just how kids are sometimes. He seemed to understand and I was able to lift his mood. After that, I gave him some of his favourite ice cream and cuddled him on the sofa while we watched some cartoons. There were no more incidents at school that I can remember, except for when he was bullied by George. I always wanted to show my kids love at a young age. I wanted them to always feel loved and supported. I know what it's like to not have anyone to support you as a youngster and I didn't want that for them.

One thing I always taught them when Emily was of age was to always be there for each other, to always support each other and love one another. I was always there for my siblings, and even though my mother abused us all, we still stood by each other. It was the only way we got through all of those years. I do feel at times that I let them down but I always tried my best to be supportive of them, to just be a big sister. I always told Bobby to be there for Emily and that he had to always protect her. She looked up to him and I knew that role was important for her growing up. Today, they are inseparable... Bobby is a few years older than Emily and I know he would do anything for her. He is a very loving older brother and he is a natural protector. I was the same with Emily but because she is a girl and younger than Bobby, I was less intense with my approach with her. Emily has a very outgoing personality. She loves to laugh and try new things. She is very boisterous and confident. I could tell from a young age that she would excel in her life. If she puts her mind to something, she will achieve it. It's just how she is.

I was really worried about my brother Timmy. At this point, he became even more distant than he usually was. He would hardly respond to my texts and rarely picked up any of my phone calls. I had no problem with that, but from a young age, I always saw a side of Timmy that concerned me. He was quite aggressive in the way that he stood up to my mother and dealt with us. It was sort of passive-aggressive. In his later years, Timmy became a recluse. When we had family meetings and outings, he would never show, and later on, would just make excuses as to why he couldn't come like he was busy with studies or had work commitments. But it was clear that he was trying to avoid being around us. He wasn't much of an uncle to my kids, not in the same way that Lizzy was an aunt to them. Our childhood had moulded him into what he had become.

One day, I was at home. Emily was asleep and Bobby was playing with his toys in his room. Tony was outside working on the garden. I put on the news just to see what the latest was. The headline was "A 23-year-old woman was found dead after being abducted in Indianapolis at a shopping centre car park." I was immediately shocked by what I was hearing. They went into more detail about what had happened. Apparently, she was just at the mall doing her shopping. A white man was spotted on CCTV coming up to her car and pushing her into the passenger's side of the car. He then got into the driver's side and drove off with her and that was the last time anyone had seen her alive. For a minute, I just sat there and I thought about my sister Lizzy. We women are very vulnerable. A lot of men take advantage of us and a lot of us are too trusting. The girl, who was named Samantha Corbyn, was 23 years old, was a mother and lived on her own in the city of Indianapolis, not far from where we were. It just astounded me that someone could do this to her in the late hours of the night. She wasn't harming anybody, she was just doing her grocery shopping, probably for her and her kids, and someone just came and took her away. She was later found and they reported that she had also been sexually assaulted, set alight and left to burn alive. It was shocking news. Her charred body was found off the interstate and just dumped there. Also, she had been reported as missing a week before. It took a minute for the news to sink in. I sat back on the sofa and turned my head to look out of the window. For a moment, I was alone again. To think about what she must have felt and what she went through got to me. I could only imagine the terror she felt when she was being raped and burned. It's dehumanising. How could someone do that to another human being? It takes a certain kind of evil to commit such a heinous crime. A real black heart and hatred for women. A man is supposed to protect a woman, so whoever this man was, he really had deep-rooted issues when it came to women, I thought. He wasn't loved or was neglected as a child. I'm no psychologist, but some of these things are easy to see. A big part of our life is our childhood. We are children for a few years and adults for the rest of our lives, so those early years can shape your life, especially if you have issues that are untreated and overlooked. I've heard of people who suffer from trauma and PTSD today because of abuse they suffered as children. I was diagnosed with PTSD. Timmy and Lizzy, however, were never diagnosed. I just prayed that they were both okay. I can imagine that they would occasionally have flashbacks and things like that because I know I did, especially in my early twenties. There were several nights when I couldn't get any sleep. I would toss and turn in my bed and just cry all night. Tony was super supportive. I don't know where I would be without him as I've said before.

The news about Samantha Corbyn stuck with me for a few days. Later on that day, when Tony had finished doing the garden up, he came inside and I made him a drink. I gave it to him but he could tell something was up when he looked into my eyes. I discussed it with him. As he always did, he made me feel safe and assured me nothing like that would ever happen to me, Lizzy or Emily. It made me feel safe when he reassured me. When we got to bed, I was still thinking about this girl. I really felt for her and her kids. I am an empath and I just felt so bad for her. I couldn't sleep; I just thought about what my mom put us through and then realised how lucky I was to still be alive. The men my mother dated never really interacted with us, so that was another fortunate thing about my childhood. Things could have been far worse, I thought.

A few days passed and again I was watching the news. I then came across a story of a woman called Sharon Peterson, a 19-year-old woman who was abducted in a car park in Kansas City. Again, she was alone, she had gone to do her shopping and was abducted in the same way. Her body was found ditched alongside the highway and she had been burned. This time, however, they found a mark on her body, on her chest; it was like a symbol or a mark that showed it was a particular person that had done it... like a signature. Again, I was shocked. I started to feel fear in my heart because a serial killer was on the prowl and he had already struck in our area and was now covering different areas across the country. They only had CCTV footage of the perpetrator but no identity or any specifics on him. He was wearing a black hat, a college jacket and blue jeans, and was of average build. I spoke to Tony about it and once again he calmed me down and made me feel safe. This world we live in is scary and no one knows how or when they are going to die. But surely one of the worst ways you can die is if you get murdered, especially being burned alive. Like the last time, this victim was also raped and then burned to death. Poor thing; she was only 19 – just a child. At the beginning of her life. She hadn't even had the chance to live and this man had robbed her of her life. It was clear that there was a serial killer on the loose. It made me think of stories about Ted Bundy, the Zodiac Killer and so many more. For the next few days, I just felt nervous every time I had to go outside of the house. Any time that I wasn't with Tony, I would feel very unsafe and vulnerable. I remember going to Walmart once and this man seemed to be following me around. He was a white man, middle-aged, had a baseball cap on and was quite tall. Every aisle that I went down he seemed to follow me. I was terrified! I suddenly stopped in my tracks, turned around and faced him. I asked him why he was following me and when I did, he would just ignore me, turn around and pretend he was looking for something on the shelves. Then, a few minutes later, he would be right back behind me. No one intervened. It was so scary. Eventually, I was so crippled with fear that I just abandoned my trolley and ran out of the store and straight to my car. I was so nervous when I got into my car that I dropped my keys on the floor and had to reach down to try and find them. I got them and nervously put them in the ignition. My hands were shaking so profusely that I could barely start the car. I looked around me and he was nowhere in sight. I drove off and kept checking my rear-view mirrors to make sure I wasn't being tailed. I wasn't. Phew! These killings put the fear of God in me and, at some point, I started to think that I would be next. I didn't return to that store again. I couldn't. From that day onwards, whenever we needed something for the house, I would ask Tony to get it or I would just go with him in my car. We had two cars – a Jeep and a Lexus.

A few weeks passed and the killer struck again. I immediately called my sister to make sure she was safe. She had told me that she hadn't been following the news and knew nothing about this killer. In a way, ignorance is bliss. Before I knew it, he had killed five victims and left his mark on all of them. The only difference was that some of them were shot and not burned. So, he was changing his MO. The unthinkable was about to happen.

Chapter 13

One day, I met up with Lizzy. I dressed up nicely. I wore a cashmere red dress and flat shoes and had my hair out. Lizzy was dressed a lot more casually – she had on some high-waisted jeans, a blue cardigan and her favourite necklace. We went for lunch in town. We had a good catch-up. She was telling me about work, her love life and her plans to become a doctor (paediatrician). She told me how many years it would take for her to become a qualified doctor, but it was something that she wanted badly and she was determined to make it happen. As I said, Lizzy was very ambitious and she knew what it was that she wanted from life. After all we had gone through, she wanted to be the change she wanted to see in others. She wanted to make a difference, not just to make a dollar. She explained to me that it was her dream and she knew it was what she was born to do. I told her that I supported her a hundred percent. It was so lovely to meet up with her. We had so many laughs and a great time together. We also discussed Timmy and his peculiar ways. I asked her if she was in regular contact with him – she frowned just as she was about to grab her cup of coffee and looked at me and said no. She told me that she had tried several times to reach out to him, but he didn't reciprocate. She told me once that she called him and they had a lengthy conversation about how he was and what his plans for his life were. What she got from that conversation was that he was a bit unsure of what he wanted to do with his life. From what I understood, Timmy wanted to go into engineering and mechanics. He was good at fixing things as I said before. It was such a shame that he had gone into himself since he had so much potential. It's just the damage that had been done by my mother that caused him to have trouble later on in life. I just figured that as he got older, he would figure things out and that It was maybe a phase he was going through. But the truth is, traumatic experiences affect people differently. No one's case is the same as another. I feel like I always gave him the impression that I was there to support him. I let him know that he could always come to me for anything.

Lizzy and I discussed the barbeque that I had and that everyone came to except Timmy. That's when I started to notice that something was amiss with him. As a child, he was very boisterous He had a big personality. If we did have a party, which we never did, he would surely have wanted to be there. I told Lizzy that it was important that we kept trying to reach out to him and that he needed our love and support and she agreed. I asked her how her boyfriend was – her face lit up and I could see the embers of joy glowing in her eyes. She told me that things were going really well between them. He wanted to become a pilot and was working towards it. From what I gleaned, he seemed to have his head screwed on and had a lot of impetus. All I truly cared about was that he treated my sister well. At the end of the day, everyone needs someone who loves them and supports them. No one wants to live life alone. When you are successful, you want to share it with that special someone. When you have a good day at work, you want to come home and tell your spouse about it. Conversely, if you have a bad day, you want to come home and have someone that can help to cheer you up. We all yearn for that love and acceptance. I knew how lucky

I was to have Tony and I wanted the same thing for my little sister. She seemed to have found a good man. When I got older, I heard so many stories about how relationships failed due to people falling out of love with each other and not sticking together. I was not going to be that person. Tony and I had gotten married about a year after the trial ended. It was a small ceremony in the local town church. It was just my siblings, Tony's brother and his parents who attended. It was a small gathering but it was beautiful and I haven't looked back since.

As soon as I left Lizzy, I contacted Timmy again. "H…h… hello," he said. He had answered this time but didn't say much – he was monotone and couldn't string a proper sentence together. There were some awkward silences on the phone and it didn't feel like I was talking to my little brother. I asked him if he was okay and he just said, "Yeah". I asked him if he needed anything and he simply said no. It wasn't much of a conversation and it left me feeling funny.

I became addicted to the news. I just kept watching it every day and wanted to hear about any developments regarding the ongoing cases surrounding the serial killer that was on the loose. There were no updates that day. About a week later, I turned on ABC News and they mentioned that they had caught the man responsible for all those killings. Before I even took a moment to see who he was, I was just relieved and immediately felt better about my safety. The news anchor kept on talking and they showed a picture of his face. I had to go into the kitchen at that exact moment so I didn't see him – I was making a cup of tea. I came back into the living room and then I heard it. His name was TIMOTHY COLLINS. I did a double take and I couldn't believe my ears. I was immediately glued to the television. I was star-ing at the screen just as they were explaining his MO and how he committed the crimes. I knew it couldn't be my brother. There was no way. They showed his face and it was my little brother Timmy. In his picture, he looked malnourished and all I could see was the same evil in his eyes that my mother had. I was in complete shock. I gasped and my jaw dropped to the floor. I was frozen stiff. I didn't know what to think. I didn't know what to say. The first thing that I did was try to call his phone. It didn't connect. Obviously. I then texted Tony who was still at work. I told him that he needed to come home as quickly as possible and that I had something to tell him. He didn't respond to my message. I was hysterical. I dropped my phone and just stared blankly through the tv. It felt like I was in a parallel universe and that it wasn't real. I kept pinching myself, hoping that I would just wake up and this nightmare would be over. I was starting to hyperventilate and I felt a panic attack coming on. I was struggling to breathe and my head felt hot, my heart was racing and my skin felt sticky. I broke out in a profuse sweat too. I just couldn't believe what was happening. I was stiff as I kept listening to the news about Timmy, my little Timmy. My head started to hurt and I just had an overwhelming feeling that I had to do something. The news person's voice started disappearing into the distance. I wasn't sure what but I needed to take action, but I was still frozen. I was sitting there alone with my thoughts. I wanted to go to Timmy's flatshare but I knew he was not there; he would be in police custody. I texted Tony again but he still didn't reply. I sat back down and couldn't move.

A few hours passed and I was still sitting on the sofa confounded and unsure of what to think or do. I couldn't tell my kids about what had happened. Emily was asleep next to me and Bobby was upstairs in his room. Tony finally came back home and I immediately ran up to him and gave him a big hug. I kept repeating the words, "He did it! He did it!" He asked me what I was talking about.

"Who did what?"

I started stuttering and couldn't get my words out.

"He killed all those women."

"Who?"

"Timmy!" I said as I burst into tears. Tony looked at me as if I had told him that the world was about to end. He was shocked too. But he asked me again what I was talking about. I explained to him that the serial killer that had been on the loose was Timmy. He couldn't believe what I was telling him. He just stood there for a second, moved backwards away from me, covered his mouth with his hands and looked down at the floor. He asked me if I was sure and I told him that they had shown Timmy's mugshot on the tv. When he finally calmed down, he tried his best to calm me down. He told me not to worry and that everything would be okay. This was as big a shock to me as it was to him. I mean, Timmy was an uncle now. The little Timmy I knew had a temper when he was young, but I wouldn't have imagined in a million years that he would have been capable of such horrible crimes. Never. Maybe it's all the years of torment that we went through and us not getting help from a professional. I started blaming myself. I told Tony that it was my fault that this had happened. I felt like I could have done more for Timmy. I asked Tony what we had to do next. He said that all we had to do was to wait until the police contacted us, seeing as I was next of kin. I had to tell Lizzy about what had happened. I picked up my phone and tried to scroll to Lizzy's number, but I was inadvertently pressing every button as I was in such a state. I finally managed to call Lizzy and told her the news. She was in complete shock; she was gobsmacked. She didn't speak for about a minute after I had convinced her that it was true. She just sat on the phone with me in silence. I called her name several times before she responded. We eventually calmed each other down on the phone and told each other that we needed to be strong to get through it. She asked me what to do next and I said I didn't know but that I assumed law enforcement would be in contact with us soon, seeing as we were his family. I asked her if she was okay and asked her if she wanted to come to my place for some time because of what had happened. She declined my offer. She told me that she couldn't watch the news that day because it was too much for her to handle. I understood.

It got a bit late and Tony and I were heading to bed. The kids were both fast asleep. I asked him to hug me tight and not let go. I felt so vulnerable and so confused all at the same time. I didn't fully understand my emotions or my thoughts. I felt anxious and restless. Somehow, I managed to fall asleep in Tony's arms and woke up around 5 am the next morning. I immediately sent an email to my boss to explain that I couldn't come to work due to a family emergency. He'd replied a few hours later to acknowledge receipt of my email. When I got up, I went downstairs and poured myself a cold glass of water. I felt a bit lightheaded so I needed to use the kitchen counter as leverage. I placed my hand on the kitchen counter and just stood there and stared out of the window at nothing. I felt numb; I couldn't believe what had just transpired. I was going to put on the tv and watch the news but I stopped myself. I went back upstairs to get my phone. I saw so many alerts. Most of them said Lizzy had called me and texted me. She was clearly panicking and she couldn't sleep. She'd sent me a barrage of messages throughout the night and the last one was just an hour before

I woke up. I walked over to the chair at the dining table and I dialled Lizzy's number. "Are you okay?" I asked. "I couldn't sleep. I'm really worried about all of this," she said. We spoke for the next hour just about the story and how shocked we were that Timmy could have done such a thing. It was like we didn't know him at all. I got off the phone with her and just sat there. Tony got up and he came into the kitchen and hugged me from behind. He asked me if I was okay and I feigned happiness. I was far from okay and he knew it. I was just putting on a brave face. He had to get ready for work but when he noticed I wasn't in bed when he woke up, he had come downstairs to look for me. I told him that I wasn't going to work. I had called in sick essentially. He understood. He asked me if I wanted him to stay with me for the day and I told him that I was going to be okay. I just needed a bit of time to come to terms with what was happening. He left for work soon after. A few hours passed and I woke the kids up, gave them breakfast and just sat with them in the living room. I wasn't taking Bobby to school. I also rang his school to inform them. Then, I heard a knock at the door. I was nervous to answer it because I kind of knew who it was. They knocked again and I got up and headed towards the door. "Who is it?" I asked, "It's the police, ma'am. Please open the door." I opened the door to see two men. One was short, stubby and looked Hispanic, while the other was tall, had a slight build and was white. I asked them what was wrong and how I could help them. They asked me if I knew a Timothy Collins. I said, "Yes." I pretended that I didn't know about what Timmy had done. They then explained that he was wanted in connection with five homicides across the country. I didn't need to act; I was in shock. Them being there made it all the more real. The shock hit me again and I just dropped to my knees and then one of the men helped me back up. I asked them what I could do for them. They asked me a couple of questions about Timmy which I answered. In the end, I also asked if I could see him and they told me that could be arranged if he decided to call me and arrange that with me. They left and I closed the door behind me. Later on, I called Lizzy to let her know that they had come to see me and that they may come to see her, so she should expect them. I also told Tony, who kept checking up on me throughout the day, and he assured me that it would be okay. I just said, "I can't believe this is happening". He said he couldn't either.

About a week passed and I received a call on the house phone. I ran to pick it up quickly and I was surprised at what I heard. "This is a collect call from Timothy Collins at Madison Correctional Facility." Timmy had called me. When I answered, he didn't sound anything like the Timmy that I knew. It was like he was a different person. Well, he obviously was; look at what he had been doing to those innocent women. Was he an incel? Why did he hate women so much? I wondered. I wanted some answers and I was going to get them. He told me that he knew I'd heard about what he had done. I just kept asking him why, why had he done it? He broke down in tears on the phone and just said he was sorry that he had disappointed me. I sighed and asked him how he could do that to innocent women and he just kept quiet and didn't respond. I needed to meet him face to face and I told him that I would come and see him the following weekend. The problem was, and this shocked me, it was likely that he would be charged with multiple charges including rape and murder and was likely to face hundreds of years in prison (multiple life sentences). I thought he may have even received the death penalty if convicted, especially in the state of Indiana. I still couldn't believe what was happening. It was all happening so fast and I felt like I was beside myself. I just wanted answers and I wanted to understand his plight.

About a week had passed and I was finding it very difficult to concentrate, especially at work. It was the day that I was going to go and visit Timmy in prison. I wanted to go alone. I did think about going there with Lizzy but I decided against that. I wanted a one-on-one with him just to gauge whether he was being truthful or not. I didn't want any interference. I went there on a Saturday. It was about noon when I arrived. I nervously stepped out of the car and my legs felt like jelly. I got to this desk where a man directed me inside to where I needed to wait to see him. He appeared before me and he looked like a caged animal. They had him in prison attire and it was like he was moving in slow motion. I couldn't believe my eyes. It felt like it was a movie. He sat down on the other side of the partition and picked up the phone. We spoke, but unfortunately, our time was limited. I asked him so many questions, but mainly, why he had done it. He couldn't speak loudly so as to not give himself up. I also asked if he was penitent and if it was something he had planned on doing, or if it was spontaneous, so to speak. From the answers that he gave me, I concluded that he was perfidious. I could see it in his eyes. I knew Timmy; from a young age, his eyes would always give him away. When he was angry or sad, he would so often lie to me and tell me that he was okay, but I could see the truth in his eyes. I believed that he intended to rape, burn and kill those women. He was just sad about the fact that he got caught. If he had the opportunity, he would probably do it again. But I still loved him; he was my little brother and he was troubled. It was entirely his fault, I thought. When I looked around and saw some of the other inmates, they looked so baleful, just dangerous, and a lot of them just had really dark energy. I felt for some of the mothers and wives who were there to see their families. It's one of the worst feelings you could ever have. It stuck with me and I will never forget it. When we got to the end of the visit. I just sat there for a minute as the guard came to take Timmy away. I didn't look up as it would have made me cry. I got home that day and Tony was asking me if I was okay and how it went. I told him that it was emotional but that Timmy didn't seem remorseful. He was broken and he was so far gone. I spent the rest of the day in and out of sleep. I was trying to do everything that I could to avoid facing reality. What scared me was the fact that I was convinced that he would receive the death penalty, and that once convicted, he would be on death row for a short period. I hate to say it but to me, Timmy didn't seem innocent. He was guilty as sin. Those poor women.

Timmy wrote a letter to me apologising for disappointing me and explaining that he was innocent. He said it wasn't him that committed those heinous crimes. I wanted to believe him but my gut told me that he was guilty. The letter made me cry because he talked about our childhood and thanked me for looking after him as a young boy. It took me back to a place that I didn't want to go to. Some time passed and the case was being televised. Lizzy and I were sequestered so we didn't see it. I couldn't believe that they were showing the trial of my little brother for the murder of five women. It was surreal. We had to testify as well. The main reason was that Timmy's lawyer wanted to give the impression that Timmy had been affected by his childhood and we had to explain how evil my mother was. That was core to the reason why Timmy had become this deranged killer. He decided to go down the 'insanity' route and believed that would be the best for Timmy's case. I was back in court again, but this time for a different reason. I was eloquent and compelling. I told them that Timmy was always a good boy and he would never hurt a fly, but the truth was, he was a grown man now and I didn't know him as well as I thought I did. I was as veracious as I could have been on the stand.

Lizzy also had to testify. She found it difficult. She would keep pausing as she started crying. In the end, dark marks from the make-up and mascara were under her eyes. The whole saga was too much for her to handle. To this day, she is still in disbelief about the case. We were honest and we said all we could. The prosecutor tore Lizzy apart to the point where the judge had to adjourn the hearing for thirty minutes before we all returned. It was hard to watch. When I looked at Timmy, he didn't seem to have much emotion on his face. Just stoic and cold. I saw the weeping families sitting in the crowd. My heart bled for them. I just thought that my brother had caused them so much pain. One of the fathers of the victims had an outburst and he yelled some obscenities at Timmy, then he was forcibly removed from the courtroom.

Timmy finally took the stand. He, like us, had to swear to tell the truth under oath. His testimony was compelling and vivid. He was torn apart by the prosecution. His story fell apart and he broke down. He admitted that he wasn't perfect and that he was anti-social but denied killing all of those women. They had DNA evidence that linked him to at least two of the murders. The evidence was overwhelming. He finally made an admission to some of the murders. He didn't have a leg to stand on. In the end, Timmy was found guilty on all counts and was sentenced to death. My heart dropped and Lizzy, Tony and I just started crying. We hugged each other and felt a deep sense of sorrow. The case was harrowing and you couldn't deny that. Timmy just had a blank stare on his face and he seemed to have accepted his fate when the verdict was read out. The jury had no sympathy for him. It was a unanimous decision. Just like that, the trial was over and my brother was known as a serial killer. Not that I had many, but I lost friends because of it, because a lot of ignorant people associate you with people you know. You are guilty by association.

For the next few days, things were very strange at home. Nothing made sense anymore, but I had to get on with things because I had been through a lot in my life. I had two kids and a loving husband so I still had a lot to look forward to. it was a dark period in my life, again. I felt so sorry for Timmy. In my mind, he was a lost little boy. If you asked me ten years ago if I thought he was capable of committing such crimes, I would have said no, absolutely not. Timmy did appeal the decision but it wasn't overturned. He was officially on death row. I saw him a few times and offered all the moral support that I could but there was nothing more I could do for him, which broke my heart. He had sealed his own fate.

About a year had passed and the day of the execution had come. I had come to terms with it all. I was nervous but I had to accept what was to come. I didn't attend the execution and neither did Lizzy. It would have broken us both. I felt bad that I couldn't be there for him in his final hour. We all wore black that day and just remembered the good things about Timmy. At this point, Bobby and Emily were a bit older and knew all about Uncle Timmy and what had happened. The house was quiet and we all just sat together for most of the day and tried our best to celebrate his life. The moment came, I felt something in my stomach and I knew it was done.

Life was depressing for a while afterwards. It took me a long time to get over it. Without the love and support of Tony, I don't know what I would have done. Lizzy and I regularly meet up today and we try our best to move on. I just keep myself busy and focus on positive things in my life. It's like distraction therapy and it works. I have been to hell and back but now I have a lot to look forward to. I miss Sally and I miss Timmy but life has to go on. At least I am now in a position where I can help people. That's the most pertinent thing.

THE END

Epilogue

This is my life story. I hope my story has helped you if you also went through or are going through some of the things that I went through. In life, we never know what hand we are going to be dealt, but we must make the best of any situation we are put in. There are always ups and downs and trials and tribulations. I never asked for any of the things that happened to me. I just had to turn things around. I couldn't have done it without the love and support of my family. At the end of the day, they are everything to me and give me a reason to live and to keep fighting. Life isn't that complicated; it's simple. You must always remember that. Even as a child, it doesn't necessarily mean you will have an easy life. You have to figure things out and always try to do the right thing. Just remember that everything that has a beginning also has an end. You won't have to suffer forever, just survive.